M000074078

Love on Ice

Olivia West

Love on Ice

Published by Olivia West

Copyright © 2019 by Olivia West

ISBN 978-1-07146-153-2

First printing, 2019

All rights reserved. No part of this book may be reproduced in any form or by any electronic or mechanical means including information storage and retrieval systems – except in the case of brief quotations in articles or reviews – without the permission in writing from its publisher, Olivia West.

www.OliviaWestBooks.com

PRINTED IN THE UNITED STATES OF AMERICA

Table of Contents

Chapter 1

To Hannah Avery, there was nothing – absolutely nothing in all of the dimensions in all of the worlds that she could possibly think of – that ever compared to the feeling of ice skating. She was a blissful hurricane on fragile ground, never intending to destroy what was around her but instead using it as a canvas for her art. It was her addiction and she loved it with all of her beating heart. It came as no surprise to anyone around her when she vowed to become a professional figure skater when she was just eleven years old. By that time, she had already been best friends with the ice rink for five years. After all, when Hannah skated, it looked like the ice was where she belonged.

Ever since the age of six, figure skating had been the biggest part of her life. She still remembered so vividly shaking at the mere thought of stepping onto the rink, with such an expansive white abyss staring at her... Hannah remembered learning about the concept "nothingness" in middle school, and to this day referred to her initial thoughts of the rink as comparable to "nothing." Her little heart beat fast and her eyes bulged out of her sockets, fearing that the whiteness was going to swallow her whole if she dipped her brand-new right skate into it. But with the encouragement of her mother, she had mustered up her courage and done it. And she never looked back.

1

One of the less brilliant things about being a figure skater was that the training schedule was pretty intense. Hannah didn't mind this, though her friends didn't always share her feelings of elation. Often, Hannah was up early and training before school as well as training straight after school. So, when she finally got home and completed her homework, she didn't much feel like the life of the party. Her friends, in an attempt to include her as much as possible in their social lives, often were left feeling like the third wheel in the relationship between Hannah and skating. It wasn't often you knew someone who excelled so much at something at such a young age, and try as they might, they just couldn't understand why every time they asked if she wanted to go out and do something, her response was always, "Sorry, guys, I'm skating later."

Throughout high school, Hannah had practiced hard, entering all sorts of amateur competitions and winning by a landslide. Her bedroom done up in pale pink was quickly turned into a silver and golden haven; you couldn't see anything for being blinded by the light bouncing off her medals lining the walls. As humble and modest as she was, she couldn't help letting her mouth form into a smirk when she was standing on those podiums, and a judge placed the medals around her neck. She knew she was the best – all skaters are trained to be the best, after all – and she felt so accomplished with her feet planted on the box with "1st" engraved upon it. She may not have been able to do algebra, but she sure kicked butt at skating!

After winning first place in one of the more well-known competitions when she was ten, Hannah had been approached by Erica Summers, a coach known for her masterful teaching style and star students. Hannah's parents had tried to get Erica to coach her before, but Erica had been too busy to take her on as a student. But after seeing Hannah's potential, Erica decided to make room in her schedule for her.

And a few years later, Hannah met Francis.

At the time, he was three years older than her, and very, *very* handsome. The crush she had developed was almost instantaneous, but unfortunately, he had never shown a similar interest in her. Francis was a fantastic skater, and his skill always motivated Hannah to try harder, to get better, and to become a skater worthy of being his partner.

And now, years later, Hannah at her tender twenty-one years of age and Francis, at twenty-four, were finally a semi-professional skating duo.

Hannah's crush was still somewhat prevalent but she had learned long ago that he wouldn't be interested in her, so she focused all her time and energy into improving her skating instead. She had secretly hoped that the feelings were simply high school Hannah's puppy love, but alas, his scruffy blond hair and

3

glorious cheekbones still put her in an annoyingly happy state.

"Hey, stop daydreaming! Break time's over!" Francis skated up to Hannah, who was leaning on the side of the rink. There was a light smile on his face, which indicated he wasn't really mad at her.

"Huh? Oh, you're *finally* here! Francis, you're late!" she chided jokingly as she pushed off the side. Her skates crossed each other in perfect synchronization as she glided around the rink, not unlike a fairy tending to her elven children up in the trees. Her light brown hair, tied back in a ponytail, flew behind her as she moved, warming up.

Francis joined her easily, wrapping an arm around her waist in the regular pair skating position. "It won't happen again. Let's practice the routine." He turned his head towards the bleachers, where Erica watched. "Music please, coach!"

***

Hannah undid the laces on her pearly white skates, her butt firmly planted on one of the benches beside the cold rink. Her heart was pounding in her chest, as she had just finished a grueling practice. She hummed the practice music under her breath, theme song from the movie version of *Romeo and Juliet*.

"Good job today." Erica sat down on the bench. "You guys really nailed that triple Salchow. Before today, you guys always were just the tiniest bit out of sync on that but you've really made it great now. If you keep that kind of pace going, I think we have a real shot at winning Snowball this year." Erica smiled warmly. Erica rarely gave out compliments without adding another critique on the end for good measure, but this time, she was really impressed. The two skaters both took a heavy but barely noticeable sigh of relief.

"I think we have a really good chance too." Hannah smiled shyly as she tugged at the hair tie, allowing her long tresses to cascade down her back. Snowball was an annual statewide competition and an incredibly big deal. Several big-name coaches and sponsors always attended, and the winners of Snowball would become internationally recognized, as well as sponsored by big companies. Hannah had always dreamed of being one of the top skaters in the professional world, and winning Snowball would be an important step on her journey to the top.

"Good job, Han," Francis said, grinning as he undid his skates next to her. "We can make it all the way. I believe in us. It all just takes a little practice." He said it in a carefree manner, but Hannah knew that underneath the loose go-with-the-flow attitude, he was serious about winning. That's what made him such a good partner.

Hannah often found Francis practicing his jumps alone in the rink, hours before practice was supposed to start. She was just as dedicated, arriving as early as he did, sometimes even earlier. But no one could compare in the way that Francis obsessed over skating, day and night. It was all he could think about. Not even Hannah knew about the way he would wake up in the middle of the night and have trouble breathing, because he was thinking about the next mistakes he would make on the ice, and what Erica would say.

"Alright, guys, I'm off. See you next practice!" Erica grabbed her bag, swung it over her shoulder, stuffed her hands in her pockets, and walked out of the rink.

Francis tapped on Hannah's shoulder as soon as Erica was gone, and gave her that smile that had melted her heart for so long. "Hey, Hannah, can I ask you something?"

Her heart beat a little faster. *Is he going to ask me out?* she wondered. But that was wildly unlikely. "Yeah, of course," she replied, slipping off her skates, putting on the protective covers, then finally stashing them in her special skating bag that her parents had bought as a commemoration of her first competition.

"I really want to try a new move. I know we've only done single and double throw axels... But I want to try a triple. I think it would really boost our marks in

6

the competition." He was willing to do whatever it took to win.

A triple axel throw was actually the most difficult throw in pair skating, and was rarely performed in competition, but it wasn't impossible, and had been pulled off before. It involved the male partner throwing the female partner, allowing her to spin three times in midair until finally landing on the ice.

Hannah was hesitant and her face showcased her unease at the proposal. "Um… It's such a dangerous move, are you sure we're ready for it? I know that we would get a lot more points, but I think we can still win with a double…"

Francis's mouth twisted into some sort of frown. He placed his hands on Hannah's arms as if to shake her into a change of heart. "That's true, but it will be much easier if we manage to pull off the triple throw axel. I think we can do it. I really do."

Staring into Francis' eyes, she felt bad for refusing to try the new move. She knew how much he wanted this, and to be honest she wanted it just as much. She wanted to please him. With a lot of extra work, perhaps she would be able to land a successful triple axel after all? Snowball was two and a half weeks away, so there was a little time. "Alright, fine."

His face lit up. "Great! I'll come earlier next practice. If you do too, we can practice it on the ground first."

It was common for figure skaters to practice their jumps and moves on the floor first, to get a feel for them, before moving onto the ice. *Thank goodness that's a thing*, Hannah thought, because it made the possibility of injury much more unlikely. Francis actually wanted to try this particular throw without Erica, as he had previously suggested this move to her but she had rejected it, believing it to be too dangerous. He was certain that Hannah would be up to the task, and wanted to try. He thought it best not to mention Erica's objections to Hannah.

"Sounds good to me!" Hannah checked her watch. She had a dinner planned with her best friend, Anya, at one of the popular new restaurants at eight o'clock. Hannah and Anya loved to try new foods, which was the reason they had become such close friends in the first place, despite their five-year age gap. It was seven o'clock now, and she still had to get home to change before going out. "Okay, I'll see you soon, Francis! I've got to get going. Bye!"

As Hannah walked away, she thought about the triple axel, and just how she was going to pull it off. The task seemed more impossible the longer she thought about it.

Chapter 2

Hannah waited in line at the local coffee shop, Java Bean, for her morning tea. She usually didn't buy tea, instead choosing to brew her own, but she had run out of tea leaves that morning. Hannah hadn't had as good a sleep as she would have liked, and was feeling too tired to forgo the caffeine. She planned on running some errands before meeting up with Anya for brunch, and she wanted to be somewhat awake for it.

As Java Bean was a fairly popular coffee café, there was a long line for drinks. Hannah waited patiently, looking at her phone. Her cute (and mildly expensive) shoulder bag hung on her body; she always took care when she wore it, as it was easily hooked onto other people's possessions.

She was just minding her own business, when someone walked past her and she felt a jolt on her body as her bag was pulled forwards by the zipper from someone's coat. "Hey!" she called out. "Stop!"

The person stopped, and turned around.

Hannah was hit by stunning crisp green eyes, a crop of luxurious dark hair, and a playful smile. She almost gasped in surprise. Wow, he was *gorgeous*! He gazed at her expectantly. Then she remembered her bag.

"Oh, my bag is hooked on your jacket!" She pointed at the zipper, and he reached down to untangle it.

"Sorry, I don't do these kinds of hookups," he smirked as he spoke in a flirty manner that instantly turned her off. It was clear in his eyes exactly what other kind of hookup he had in mind. No matter how attractive he was, it was annoying when men had too much of an ego and just assumed all women were going to sleep with them.

"You wish," Hannah muttered under her breath as she headed back to her place in line, apologizing to the person who had originally been behind her.

The man passed her again on his way out. He was holding one of the carryout boxes, and she assumed he had been picking up an order. He caught her eye, and shot her a wink and a smile; she didn't return it at all. In fact, it made her shudder.

Though he had gone, he lingered in Hannah's thoughts for a brief moment more as the line moved ahead. He was strikingly attractive, but the large ego he had shown was just too much. Hannah pushed him from her mind as she stepped up to the cash register. "Hi, one medium black tea, please."

***

Hannah arrived at the rink, fully stretched out and prepared.

Hannah had made sure to exercise plenty earlier to keep her body loose and limber. Having a flexible body was essential to making successful jumps, and Hannah wanted to make sure she was as prepared as possible for the triple axel throw. In her apartment, she had already done some practice jumps. She hoped the people in the apartment below her weren't too annoyed!

Hannah hummed a song as she walked. She was in a very good mood after brunch with Anya. The taste of the delicious spinach quiche she had ordered still lingered on her tongue. Her sleek brown hair was tied back in a ponytail, like usual.

Hannah slipped into the women's changing room. She changed from her thick winter coat and scarf to her practice leotard. Her snow-white skates replaced her favorite black flats. She always felt a surge of affection whenever she put them on, and delighted in the fact that she was going to be skating soon.

After locking her personal items away, Hannah headed to the rink.

It was empty, as many of the skaters that frequented this rink were in school at this time of the day. There were many budding teenage skaters that Hannah liked to watch skate, for they were so nimble on the ice, but they weren't here now.

She pushed open the big door and stepped onto the ice.

Her body soon grew warm as she glided around the rink, doing circles, spins, and step sequences. She practiced her spins, particularly the triple axel. She was delighted to see that she could still do the spin gracefully and land perfectly. But it was much harder when it was a throw.

"Hannah!" She heard a call and turned around. She saw it was Francis, at the edge of the rink, preparing to skate out and join her.

"Hey!" she called back.

"Are you prepared for the throw?" he asked as soon as he was beside her. "I'm excited to try it!"

"Shouldn't we try it on the ground first?"

"Yeah, of course. Sorry, I got ahead of myself!" He laughed. "Let's go."

The pair made their way out of the rink. They slipped off their skates and stood in their thick socks on the black floor. "Okay, here we go."

"Let's start with a single," Hannah suggested.

Francis nodded before he put his hands on her waist and threw her into the air, watching her spin her body once in a tight whirl. She landed on the ground, feet flat, planted firmly.

"Okay, on to double," he told her, going through the same motions, this time watching Hannah spin two times before she landed smoothly on the ground once more.

"Now for the hard one." Hannah grimaced as she prepared herself, taking steadying breaths.

Francis threw her as high into the air as he possibly could. Hannah felt the rush of adrenaline. Then she spun, one, two, and three... before she stumbled on the landing. "Crap," Hannah muttered to herself as she steadied. "Sorry, that was a horrible end," she called out, louder.

"It's okay! Let's just practice again." Francis grinned.

Fifteen minutes later, Hannah had finally been able to make a great end pose.

"Are you feeling ready to try it on the ice?" Francis asked as he led her back to the rink. "We've got a couple minutes before Erica gets here, we can try it out and see if we can do it."

Though she was a little nervous about it, Hannah did want to improve and not let Francis down. She never wanted to let Francis down.

So, she followed him onto the ice. They skated like before, getting warmed up and used to the feeling of being on ice. Though being off the ice felt weirder for Hannah. There was nothing more comforting than feeling the rush of icy wind as she circled the rink... her very own indoor winter wonderland that only the most privileged got to experience.

Like before, they started with a single, then upgraded to a double. Then, before she knew it, it was time to try the triple.

Her heart pounded as he put steadying hands on her waist. "Here we go..." he murmured as they glided in perfect synchronization.

Her palms were sweaty despite the freezing temperature of the rink, but she still continued to prepare for the move.

Then he lifted her up, and threw.

Her body didn't leave the ice right. She wasn't sure how, but it felt different from the usual times they practiced. Maybe it was nerves, she didn't know.

A pang of shock ran through her body, sending her into a panic.

Her feet found themselves tangled together, and her body felt too heavy to move. She tried sending herself into a spin, but it didn't work. Her arms flailed wildly. She couldn't spot properly. She was falling... falling... *No!* she screamed furiously in her thoughts as she hurtled towards the ice dangerously.

Then there was nothing but pain, and the world turned to black.

***

Hannah lay on her back, staring up at the vast ceiling of the skating rink, feeling cold spread throughout the upper half of her body. *Why am I lying here?* She thought. *I'd better get up.* But when she tried to move her legs, a shot of pain traveled through her.

"Ah-ouch!" She winced.

"Hannah? HANNAH!" She became aware of Francis at her side, kneeling, touching her arm. She turned her head slightly to look at him with wide, unblinking eyes. Everything felt so surreal.

Though she didn't know it at the time, Hannah was in a state of shock. Her body seized up as shudders ran through her.

"Francis? What's wrong?" Erica's voice rang out across the rink. She had just arrived at the rink at the regularly scheduled practice time. She had seen Francis crouching over Hannah, and was immediately on high alert.

"Hannah's hurt!" Francis yelled back. He watched as Erica walked onto the ice with her sneakers. There was no time to borrow skates, and she was incredibly worried about Hannah. She walked, but really more like slid unsteadily across the ice towards the two.

"What happened?! Is it serious?!" Erica had focused all her time and energy into training Hannah, and didn't believe that Hannah could fall this badly without special circumstances. Hannah was a careful person, who always knew what her limits were, and knew when she was going too far. How could this have happened?

"E-Erica…?" Hannah muttered as Erica's worried face came into her view.

"You just hold on, Hannah… I'm going to call an ambulance!" Erica pulled out her smartphone and dialed 9-1-1. She stood and stared at Hannah's twisted body, with one leg at an odd angle. It was clearly broken, and possibly worse. "Damn it…" Erica cursed under her breath as her phone rang. "Hello? I need an ambulance!" she said as soon as an operator picked up.

Francis listened to Erica give the operator the details. He kneeled down and realized that the best course of action was to wait for the ambulance but keep Hannah warm. He grabbed his coat to cover her and held her hand tightly as they waited.

Minutes later, the roar of the ambulance could be heard. Paramedics poured into the rink, pushing a stretcher. "It's a good thing we were nearby, thanks to that false alarm," one of the paramedics said to the other. "It looks like a bad break. Lift her onto the stretcher on the count of three. One… two… three!"

The two men lifted her slim body onto the pure white stretcher.

"We're going to go to Hope Hospital. We can't let you ride in the ambulance, but you're welcome to come see her after the doctor's diagnosis and possible surgery," the second paramedic explained to Francis and Erica, who nodded in understanding.

Hannah looked up from the stretcher. "SURGERY? But I have figure skating practice!"

"Well, it looks like you're going to have to skip practice today, miss," one of the paramedics said.

"Francis, we should go to the hospital immediately," Erica said.

"Agreed."

Francis and Erica watched as the paramedics wheeled Hannah out onto the ambulance. Minutes later, they drove away, sirens blaring. Erica and Francis followed, both of them hoping that Hannah would be alright, but both for slightly selfish reasons.

Chapter 3

Everything was blindingly white when Hannah opened her eyes.

Where am I? she wondered as her vision cleared, and realized that she was in a room of sorts, with a beeping sound that was somewhat calming. Hannah looked towards her right, and saw an IV bag. *Hospital...* Then she remembered the accident. *My leg!*

Hannah tried to lift her leg but realized it was much heavier than usual. "Ugh..." She groaned as she attempted to lift her head to see why. Her leg was completely covered with a thick white cast, which prevented her from moving much.

"Oh, Hannah, you're awake!" Erica, who had fallen into a light sleep while waiting for Hannah to awake, was alerted by her groan. Erica stood up and rushed to Hannah's side, examining her. "How are you feeling? The morphine should dull the pain."

"E-Erica..." Hannah smiled weakly, appreciative that her coach had stayed. "Where's... Francis?"

"He's just getting a snack. He should be back soon..." Erica looked towards the door, which promptly opened. "Speak of the devil!"

"Hey, Hannah, you're awake!" Francis said as he held out a pack of chips from the vending machine. "Feeling hungry?"

Just before Hannah could answer, the door swung open again, and a man in a sweeping, long white coat entered the room. "Ah, Ms. Avery, I'm glad to see you're awake. I'm your doctor, Dr. James."

Hannah sat up as best as she could. "Do you have good news, Dr. James?"

"Well, I'll put this as gently as I can, Hannah. Your leg was broken very badly. It was at an awkward angle when you fell, and while it is stable now, it will take a long time to heal. And even if it does... At this stage, it's impossible for us to determine if you will be able to skate the same as before. And... there is a possibility that you may not ever be able to skate again, if it doesn't heal correctly."

Hannah felt like she had fallen all over again. That image that she first had of the ice rink when she was six years old – the nothingness that she thought was going to swallow her whole – just came true.

"N-never skate again?" she repeated, feeling like her heart had dropped into the pit of her stomach and into the nothingness with the rest of her body.

Erica looked completely appalled. "How is this possible? She's one of my best skaters! We have a competition soon that we've been practicing so hard for!"

"There's nothing we can do about it, except pray for the best. If she tries any strenuous activity too soon, it may jeopardize her leg properly healing. And we can't have that." The doctor took another look at Hannah's charts. "I'm sorry, Ms. Avery."

Hannah's eyes were wide open, and she couldn't think. If she never skated again… What else could she do? Skating had been her whole life since she had been a child. There was nothing she wanted more than to skate for the rest of her life.

"I'll let you have some time to yourself," Dr. James said, realizing that she probably needed time to process the devastating information that he had just given her. "I'll come check on you in the evening." The doctor left the room, leaving Hannah alone with Erica and Francis.

Francis still hadn't talked, and was looking like he was lost in thought. About what, Hannah didn't know. "We should probably give Hannah some space, Francis. Her parents will be here soon anyway." Erica shook him back to the present. "We'll come back later, Hannah. Get some rest." Erica squeezed Hannah's hand gently.

"Thank you, Coach. See you soon." Hannah waited until they had gone before collapsing onto her pillow.

"Damn it…" She glared at her leg. "Why did I ever agree to try that move in the first place?" She couldn't help feeling like it was all Francis' fault that the accident happened. Not that she blamed him completely, because it was her own choice to take to the ice and attempt the move with him, but she was angry that he had the audacity to look like she had let him down on her own.

She looked up at the ceiling, trying not to think about her future. It loomed over her now, scary, and uncertain. Hannah's heart pounded as she took deep breaths, trying to calm herself down. She decided that at this point, getting some rest would be the best option, though she couldn't stop the tears from rolling down her heavy cheeks.

Hannah blocked all the negative thoughts and instead replayed classical music in her head, songs that she had used for practices for previous competitions, for they always calmed her down. And before long, she was drifting into a deep, dreamless sleep.

***

Hannah awoke in the afternoon feeling groggy, but better than the night before. She propped herself up, suddenly aware that her stomach was growling. She hadn't eaten anything in a while, and wondered when she would be getting food next.

Looking to her right, she discovered a bouquet of flowers and a teddy bear. And a card. *Who's this from?* she wondered with a smile as she picked up the card. As she scanned it, she realized it was from Anya. *She's so sweet,* Hannah thought with a smile. She felt blessed to have such a great friend in her life.

She continued to read the card, but her head snapped up when the door opened. "Anya?" Was she still around?

"Nope, just me." Francis stepped into the room with a look on his face that was like a hesitant smile. "How are you feeling?"

"Better than yesterday, that's for sure. Just... worried about my leg, I guess. I miss skating already, and it's only been a day... I can't even imagine how tough the next months are going to be." She put a smile on her face, determined to remain positive. She had decided that there was no use thinking about worst-case scenarios. "I'm really wishing to heal quickly. I can't wait to get back onto the ice."

"Actually, Hannah, skating is what I wanted to talk to you about," Francis sighed as he sat down on the side of her bed and gazed into her eyes.

"Yeah, sure, what's up?"

"I've been giving this a lot of thought, and..." He trailed off, leaving a concerned look on Hannah's face.

"Francis, what? What's wrong?"

"I can't be your partner."

Hannah's face turned into one of relief, and she awkwardly laughed. "You mean for Snowball, right? Since my leg's hurt? Well, yeah, of course! You don't have to be so dramatic about it. Once I heal, we'll be back on track for the rest of the competitions in no time!"

"No, Hannah, I can't be your partner for anything, from this point on."

There was a pause.

"Francis... Come on, this isn't funny." Bewilderment showed clearly on her face.

He sighed heavily. "I'm serious, Hannah. It's just... hearing the doctor talking about how you might never skate again, or how you'll never be the same... I don't think you'll be as strong a partner for me, and I need to move on, Hannah. I can't wait around for the possibility that you'll be fully healed. I have a lot of ambition, and I need to be moving forwards."

"Ambition? So do I, Francis! It was just a mistake that I fell on that throw. But I know I can do better! Once I heal—"

"No, Hannah, I've made up my mind. I can't wait for you to heal. I need to keep practicing, and improving. Time is of the essence. Please, understand."

"Yeah, I understand *perfectly*." Hannah's tone turned icy now, as she glared at him. They had been partners for so long, and she had considered them good friends. Now his true colors were showing. She knew that she could train until she was as good as she had been before. It just would take some time.

But Francis' drive wouldn't allow him to stop. "I'm really sorry, Hannah. But I just can't see another way for me. Snowball and other competitions are coming up soon and…" He didn't want to say it, but was thinking that if she couldn't do a triple axel throw, he needed a partner who could.

The thought had already come to her, and she struggled to hold back the tears that threatened to surface. "Well, I can't stop you, Francis." She knew that no matter what she said, she wouldn't be able to change his mind. He was just too damn stubborn.

He was beginning to feel slightly guilty, though he had already convinced himself the night before that this was for the best. He had himself to think about. Swallowing nervously, Francis ran a hand through his cropped hair. "I'm sorry."

"Leave." She took a deep breath as she lay back onto the pillow, closing her eyes. "And don't come back."

Without another word, Francis got up. Hannah felt the pressure from his side of the bed disappear, and after the door clicked shut, she let go.

Tears streamed down her face, as sobs wracked through her body. Her future had been taken away from her, in an instant, and because of one move. One mistake. *I never should have agreed to try the throw. Never.* She hated that aspect of herself, the one that wanted to please everyone.

"Damn it, how did things end up like this?" She had devoted her whole life to skating. The reality that she might never skate again was really sinking in now, and she couldn't help but cry, as she felt so completely lost.

The door slid open again, and Hannah yelped as she drew the covers over her body. "Go away, Francis, didn't I tell you I never wanted to see you again?" She didn't want anyone seeing her like this, weak and tearful. Especially not *him*.

"Han? It's just me!" Anya hurried to Hannah's bed, and put a hand on the bundle of blanket. "Are you okay?"

Anya gently pulled back the blanket and her brow furrowed as she looked into the tear-filled eyes of her best friend. "Han…" she murmured quietly. She didn't ask what had happened, or why Hannah was crying. She simply reached down and hugged Hannah. "Cry it all out, sweetie. Just let it all out…"

Chapter 4

The doctors said Hannah was recovering remarkably, better than they had ever predicted. They delivered this happy news to her a week after she had entered the hospital, which only cheered her up a little. She would be discharged in a matter of days, and the doctors expected her to make a good recovery, if not full.

Though she was glad that she would ultimately be able to skate again after her leg healed, she knew that even if she were completely healed, she would have no partner, and no coach. But the reality of being able to skate made her feel much better.

As Hannah ate her hospital breakfast, which really wasn't as bad as all the rumors made it out to be, the door to her room slid open, revealing Anya, who had a big smile plastered on her face. "Morning, Han!"

"Morning, Anya. What's got you so happy?" Hannah smiled as she took in Anya's sleek business dress that clung to every part of her body, showing off her slim figure. She had no idea how Anya managed to find time to exercise so vigorously while still getting all her work done.

"Well... I have some good news for you! So you know how... you broke your leg?" Anya started with a joke, making Hannah laugh.

"How can I forget?"

"Well, you might as well earn some money while you rest that leg, and since I don't want you moping around your apartment all day missing skating, I found something to keep your mind off it." Anya took a breath for dramatic effect. "I got you a job!" she finally announced, her face all smiles.

Hannah's eyebrows raised in surprise. "Really? As what?"

"As a temp for my law firm!" Anya grinned. "It's the perfect job for you."

"I don't know if I could do a good job, though..." Hannah murmured. She practically knew nothing about law.

"Han, seriously, you'd be great. Plus we really need the help. Three of our paralegals just left. Two poached, one with family issues. You have a degree in writing, and you took like six months of pre-law." Anya picked up a piece of orange from Hannah's tray. Knowing Hannah didn't like them, she popped it into her mouth.

"Only six months before I decided figure skating would be a better choice!"

"Come on, it's just filing papers, checking over documents, and things like that. Besides, you've watched so much *Law & Order*, you might as well have a degree." Anya laughed as she ate another piece of orange.

Hannah began to realize that Anya was right. She did need a distraction from her injury, and she couldn't just sit on her behind for months while she healed. "Alright, Anya, I'll do it." Hannah grinned as she squeezed her best friend's hand with affection.

"Fantastic!" Anya polished off the rest of the orange slices. "Now, when are you going to be discharged? I bet you're sick of all the hospital food and oranges. And I miss having someone to shop with!" At Hannah's humorously raised eyebrows, Anya laughed. "You know I'm just joking. I know you're going to need your rest." Now her expression turned somber. "I really hope you can skate again as soon as possible, Han."

"The doctors say I can be discharged in a couple of days. But I'm going to need crutches for sure for a while. Still, it's better than just staying in the hospital."

"Of course. Do you want to stay with me?" Anya suggested. "I want to help as much as I can!"

"I think I'll be alright. There's an elevator in my building, and I've got your number if I ever need help. Thanks for offering, though. You're the best."

The door opened, and the nurse walked in. "Good morning, Hannah. How are you feeling?"

"Much better, thanks, Nurse Joyce."

Anya checked her watch. "Oops, I'd better get back to the office. I took a little break to come see you, but it's almost over. I'll text you, okay?"

"Okay. See you later." Hannah nodded, and Nurse Joyce smiled. It was important for a recovering patient to have a good support system, and it looked like Anya was just that. As were Hannah's parents.

But her parents didn't sneak a tea from Java Bean into the hospital and leave it in the bedside drawer so the nurse couldn't see it before winking and leaving the room like Anya did.

"You're doing really well, Hannah!" Nurse Joyce exclaimed happily as she checked the medical chart. "Are you ready for your discharge soon?"

"More than ready," Hannah nodded as she finished the last scoop of her scrambled eggs and watched as Joyce took the tray. "Thank you, so much."

"No problem, dear. Get some rest!" Joyce left the room in a good mood, humming a tune.

Hannah did as she was told, and lay down on the pillow, dreaming of being out on the ice again, skating.

***

Several days later, Hannah was released from the hospital with a cast and crutches, as she had predicted. It was weird for her at first, but Nurse Joyce had sweetly taken the time to train her. Step by step, they had made it down the long hallway of the hospital, with Joyce making sure that Hannah kept steady the whole time. All she could think about, however, while this was happening, were the training stages of her figure skating and the likeness it had to this experience.

"Now, honey, if you just hold on to my arm… that's it…"

Hannah had been going to the ice rink for a few weeks, and her trainer Susan thought it was time to try a waltz jump. It was still difficult to stay balanced on the ice but Susan ensured both Hannah and her parents that she was far more advanced than "normal" students.

"But what if I fall, Miss Susan?" Hannah cried.

"Then you fall, my dear. But then you'll get back up, thankful for the invention of butt pads even if they make you look a lil' chunky, and you'll try the move again. Now, lift your right leg — that's it — and push off on your left toe pick…"

"I landed it! I did it!" Hannah said, elated with the result of her efforts.

"Brilliant, honey. You're doing really well."

It was now in the late afternoon, and the sun was beginning to set as Hannah gathered her things, making sure not to forget to pack her favorite book, *Alice in Wonderland*. It was the way that Alice was thrown into this new world and made the best of it that Hannah admired. She did a final check, then swung her shoulder bag over her body. Grabbing her crutches, Hannah made her way to the door. She was just about to attempt to open it when it opened of its own accord.

"Oh, Hannah!" Nurse Joyce smiled brightly as Hannah took a step back in surprise, usurping her balance. "Careful!" she warned as she helped Hannah back onto her feet and into the wheelchair that the hospital required all patients to leave in.

"Ah, I'm such a klutz," Hannah said as she grimaced. "Thank you so much."

"It's no problem at all, Hannah, it's my job after all," Joyce laughed as she cheerfully spoke. "You're getting discharged! Congrats!"

"Yeah, I am," Hannah said as Joyce wheeled her out into the hallway.

"Is someone coming to pick you up?" Joyce asked as she and Hannah slowly made their way down the corridor, heading towards the hospital exit.

"Anya should be here anytime..." Hannah said as they reached the exit. They made small talk as they waited for Anya to arrive.

The doors opened and Anya clacked in. "Hey, Han, ready to go?"

Hannah gave Nurse Joyce a warm hug. "Good luck, darling." Joyce grinned. "I have to get back to work. Have fun!"

"Thank you for everything, Joyce!" Hannah stood up with a smile and held onto Anya, who helped Hannah to her car. "So my first day is next Monday?"

"Nope, actually the Monday after that. I thought you shouldn't start too soon, and should give your leg some more rest, so I talked to the hiring manager. Are you excited?" Anya's eyes twinkled as she drove towards Hannah's apartment.

"A little. But also very nervous. What if I don't do well?" Hannah mused as she thought about all the potential disasters that could occur.

Anya shook her head playfully. "Don't worry, Hannah. You're going to do so well!" she said, intent on making sure Hannah's worries were dispelled.

"I'm sure my parents will be proud of me for doing something worthwhile for the first time in my life."

"They're always proud of you, Han," Anya chuckled. "Do you think they'd pay that downtown ice rink thousands of dollars a year if they weren't proud of you?"

That put a smile on Hannah's face. "Oh yeah, you've got a point!"

Ten minutes later, Anya smoothly pulled up to Hannah's building. She came to a stop, parked, and helped Hannah up to her apartment. Once she was sure that Hannah didn't require more assistance, she left.

But not without saying, "God, you're so heavy these days, Han… did you steal extra servings of hospital food?" before winking and backing out of the doorway.

Hannah sat in her comfy armchair as she smiled, thinking that she was quite lucky to have such a great best friend like Anya. She found herself genuinely looking forward to next Monday, and the new challenges that the law firm would bring. Allowing those thoughts to fill her head, Hannah washed up and crawled into bed, where she soon fell fast asleep.

Chapter 5

On the appointed Monday morning, Anya arrived at Hannah's door bright and early. She all but bounded in once Hannah had opened the door, her stylish dark bob of hair bouncing as though it had its own lease on life. "Are you all ready to go?" she said as she took in Hannah's outfit.

Hannah had picked out a professional-looking maroon blazer paired with a classic little black dress, pulled together with a white scarf. She looked absolutely fantastic. Anya couldn't keep her lips together as she smiled at how great Hannah looked, even if she had a hard white cast on. Hannah had opted for comfy flats today, and leaned on her crutches as she grinned at Anya. "Do I look good enough?

"Good enough? You look *perfect*." Anya giggled in delight. "But how do you feel? How's your leg?"

"It's getting a lot better. I'm going to go to the doctor soon for another checkup, but the last time, he said that I'm healing really well. Some patients have taken six months to heal, but he's optimistic that I'll be able to heal in three or so."

"Wowie, missy, you're just perfect at everything, aren't you!" Anya teased. "First ice skating, then miracle bone-healing. Pretty soon you're going to beat me at my own law game!"

"Haha, very funny!" Hannah retorted. "I know nothing about law."

"You always seem to forget you went to, and quit, law school."

"I tend not to be a big fan of talking about my failings in life! And by the way, that's one activity on the list of things-I'm-not-perfect-at."

"Oh damn, there is one thing after all. You know another thing you could put on that list right now?" Anya said.

"What?"

"Walking!"

Hannah rolled her eyes and the two friends burst into uncontrollable laughter. By the time they could breathe properly again, Anya had tears streaming down her face and Hannah's ribs hurt from laughing so much. And for the first time in a while, not a single thought about figure skating consumed Hannah's mind.

***

When Hannah arrived at the law firm, she was slightly overwhelmed.

Lawyers and litigators were everywhere, looking very professional. She felt out of place, but Anya was determined that Hannah not feel awkward. She led Hannah towards the elevator, where they would ride to her floor. Many successful-looking men and women greeted Anya on the way. She was obviously well respected here. Hannah felt impressed by Anya, who was an incredible lawyer.

Though she was only twenty-six, she had been picked up by Meyers & Brown right after graduating from law school and quickly rose through the ranks due to her smarts. Anya often told Hannah how opposing lawyers had underestimated her, judging her purely by her appearance, and how she had used that against them. Just recalling the memories almost made Hannah laugh to herself, which she thankfully held back at the last second.

Once they had reached Hannah's cubicle, Anya explained Hannah's duties. "Alright, Han, I tried to get the temp job with the least about of manual labor like copying, so all you have to do is go through these files and make sure they're all up to date, and such," Anya said as she subtly pointed to a stern-looking woman sitting in her tiny office. "When you're finished with that, ask Helen what you should do next. If you need me, just call, okay? Oh, and the best part, you get an hour-long lunch break!"

"Whoa, that's more than I ever get at the rink."

Anya squeezed Hannah's hand. "You are going to be so comfortable here, Han. Plus you get to be lazy and earn money for it at the same time!"

"Can we grab something to eat together?" Hannah asked hopefully.

Anya frowned, her bottom lip pushing outwards and her brows furrowing. "Sorry, I can't today. I have a meeting and some important files to prepare. But you can go get lunch in any of the shops on the street, there are some really great bistros – and also some fast food if you want to be unhealthy." Anya chuckled. "I really recommend the organic café though." Anya's phone beeped, prompting her to check it. "Oh, damn, Meyers needs me. I'll talk to you later, Han. Good luck!"

Hannah turned to her desktop, determined to get into the groove of things. She was going to do her absolute best at this, and try to forget about life on the ice as much as humanely possible. Blocking out all the outside noise, Hannah began to focus.

***

Before long, lunchtime seemed to roll around. Hannah hadn't even noticed that it was twelve, and was only alerted by a sudden uprising of people getting up from their seats. She was just about to text Anya when she remembered that Anya had a meeting. *I guess I'll take Anya's advice and go check out the bistros.*

She swung her bag over her shoulder, and grabbing her crutches, headed towards the elevator.

A little while later, Hannah found herself in front of a charming little organic café, the Loose Leaf. She had always liked organic food, but it seemed like the place was incredibly full. She waited in line anyway, and eventually was able to score herself a delicious-looking sandwich, chock full of spinach, eggs, and fat-reduced mayonnaise.

Since all the seats were taken in the café itself, Hannah was forced to take her sandwich and find another place to sit. She continued to walk at her slow pace, and found a clear bench. Smiling, Hannah sat down and took a deep breath. *Oh man, even walking is tiring me out these days,* she thought.

Just as she was beginning to peel apart the wrapping on her sandwich and take her first bite, she heard a familiar sound.

The scraping of a blade on ice.

Hannah's head shot up as she recognized the sound, realizing that she was sitting near an outdoor ice rink. An overwhelming wave of emotion threatened to engulf her, as she remembered her skating days and how Francis had left her. She missed skating so much, and all she wanted to do was skate for the rest of her life – not sit in an office in a law firm. Not really.

Her future had been so bright, but it had all been snatched away from her in an instant. It would be so hard for her to get back into the professional world without a caring partner and a coach to stop her from making those dreadful mistakes that caused her to fall in the first place. Hannah shook her head as she turned her head away from the skating rink, not wanting to think about the terrifying future.

She lowered her head and ate again, focusing on her sandwich while trying to ignore the stinging feeling in her eyes, and concentrating on thinking about work and all of those important documents that need to be completed for that afternoon. The lunch hour passed quickly, and before long, Hannah was back at her desk, tapping away on the computer.

It wasn't the most exciting of jobs, as compared to being on the ice, but she made do. She had to make do, or the memories of skating would drive her crazy.

When five o'clock hit, she looked up to find Anya at her cubicle. "Hey, An."

"Made it through your first day alright?" Anya smiled widely. "Sorry, I couldn't come visit you, this day's been so busy for me."

Hannah thought about the ice skating rink, and wondered if Anya had known about it. She supposed that Anya probably did, but probably wanted to spare Hannah by not telling her. So she didn't mention it either. "I'm all in one piece. Well, almost in one piece for someone with a broken leg! I'm so tired though, want to get some dinner?"

Anya grinned brightly. "Of course. Let's go!"

Chapter 6

As the weeks passed, Hannah dedicated herself to the law firm, working to the best of her abilities. Her leg felt better and better and as time passed she found herself relying less on the crutches, much to her delight. Soon, it had been almost a month and a half since the incident.

Though Hannah still missed skating with all her heart, she found that having the time to sit down and work was quite relaxing, and definitely allowed her leg to heal. Though at first she had been avoiding the ice rink near the office, she had recently started to watch some of the young skaters practice.

It did make her heart burn with sadness that she couldn't skate again yet, but there was some comfort in watching kids skate – their fresh bones and unbruised arms and eyes ravenous for more time on the ice as soon as they were told to take a break.

Hannah had read in the local paper that Francis had won Snowball with his new partner Lucy, a promising young girl who had been training just as hard as Hannah. The papers had marvelled in the fact that they had only been together for a couple weeks before being able to win the competition.

It had hit her hard, but not as hard as it would have been three weeks earlier. It did make her wonder whether or not she wanted to skate again professionally. Even if she wanted to, she wasn't sure if she would be good enough to beat Francis and his new partner. These thoughts weighed heavily on her mind almost all the time.

"Hannah Avery?" The pretty blonde receptionist called Hannah's name, snapping her out of her thoughts. Hannah had been sitting in the waiting room. "Please follow Nurse Joyce."

Nurse Joyce appeared in front of Hannah, full of smiles. "So great to see you again, Hannah! How's my favorite ice skater feeling?" Joyce walked slightly in front of Hannah as they made their way down the hallway, heading towards a room.

"Much better, thank goodness. How are you?" Hannah said, returning the question.

"Just fine, thank you. Busy, busy, busy, as usual. Ah, here we are." Joyce led Hannah into a big room with a lot of complicated machinery scattered about. "We're just going to take some quick x-rays. It'll only take a couple of minutes!"

After the x-ray, Joyce brought Hannah to an exam room with a crisp white bed, where Hannah was gently directed to sit. "Doctor James will be right in to discuss your x-rays. Hope everything goes well!"

She gave Hannah a light hug before pulling away. "See you later, my little skater!"

Hannah relaxed as she sat on the bed, waiting for the doctor's arrival. Minutes later, the door slid open. "Ah, Hannah! Feeling better?" Doctor James' smiling face popped into the doorway and the rest of the man followed soon after. He walked to Hannah's side, and inspected the cast.

"I think I'm doing a lot better. The leg doesn't really ache anymore, and it's not just thanks to the meds." Hannah smiled as she tucked a lock of her hair behind her ear. It was much harder to explain the aching inside of her that missed skating.

Dr. James paced over to the backlight machine, where he read the x-rays for a couple minutes. "Good news, Hannah! Everything looks just in order. In fact, you're healing quite quickly. The break is setting really well. I think you might be able to take off those crutches in several weeks."

"Great! Do you think I'll be able to skate soon?" She asked the question that she had been pondering for a long while.

"Well, what's going to happen first is that once we're sure your leg will be able to heal successfully, we're going to remove your crutches and replace your hard cast with one that will allow you to walk while still keeping your leg secure. After that, we can evaluate whether or not you'll be able to skate," Dr. James explained.

"Okay, I understand." She smiled, feeling more at ease.

"But I'm really optimistic, Hannah. Don't worry, I'm sure you'll be back on the ice in no time." Dr. James grinned, while Hannah's spirits lifted.

She moved off the bed and nodded. "Thank you so much, Dr. James."

The doctor's cell phone began to beep, prompting him to pick it up off his belt. "Oh, okay, I have to go. I'll see you soon, Hannah! Take care." Dr. James all but dashed out of the room, no doubt hurrying off to whatever emergency he had been called to. Hannah slowly made her way out of the hospital.

Her phone rang, and she checked it, delighted to see that it was Anya, ready to pick Hannah up from her appointment to go to dinner. Putting skating from her mind, Hannah headed towards the hospital exit, looking forward to having a good time with her best friend.

***

Hannah was on the ice again, gliding as gracefully as an angel. She performed every trick and jump perfectly, landing back on the ice amid cheers from the watching audience. It made her smile with every perfect move.

She felt like she was on cloud nine, like she was able to do anything in the world if she wished it. There was never a feeling like it.

The music ended, and Hannah came to a stop, throwing her hands triumphantly into the air as the crowd roared around her.

An announcer's voice boomed throughout the rink. "Ladies and gentlemen, that was the amazing Hannah Avery! Is there even any need to deliberate about who the winner of the world's best skater competition is? Give her a round of applause!"

The audience began to clap again, and Hannah beamed happily as she began to do a victory lap around the rink. The lights dimmed and from the side, the entrance to the ice opened and Francis skated out.

"Introducing... the fantastic Francis Miller!"

Francis joined Hannah and slid his hands around Hannah's waist as they skated with perfect synchronization. They felt like they were meant to be resting there until the end of time. "Let's do it," he whispered into her ear.

"What? I'm not ready!" she protested, flailing her hands frantically.

Francis didn't answer, but lifted Hannah in the air and threw her high. She let out a yell as she hurtled towards the ground, bracing for the impact. But it never came.

The ground beneath her disappeared, swallowing her whole as she fell, further and further down with no end in sight. She was

gaining speed, and looking down, the ice suddenly appeared.
"No, no, no, no, NO!" she cried out as she steeled her body for
the explosive burst of pain.

***

Hannah sat up in the darkness, drenched in a cold sweat. She panted heavily as she struggled to breathe. The dream had seemed so real. It echoed in her mind as she swept matted hair away from her face. "Damn it," she muttered as she slowed her breathing, calming herself down.

The dream terrified her.

The first part had been so good, the part she missed the most, skating on the ice without a care in the world. But now the fall marred her memory, scarring her. She realized just how scared she was about skating again, but she still remembered how much she wanted to be back on the ice.

Hannah checked her phone, realizing it was seven thirty in the morning. *No point in going back to sleep.* She had work soon anyways. She got up, heading towards the shower.

The hot spray felt so good as it washed away the last remaining memory of the dream, and it was a relief to know that at least she was clean on the outside. The jealousy towards Francis' new partner, the pent-up rage she felt towards Francis for dumping her (quite literally), and the melancholy of being away from the ice for too long... that would be harder to erase.

After putting on makeup and getting dressed, Hannah hailed a taxi to the office, arriving just on time. "Good morning, Hannah!" an associate greeted her happily.

"Morning, Margaret!" Hannah said back before sliding into her cubicle. It was time to bury herself with work until lunchtime, like any usual day. She was finding the work interesting, and didn't mind the long hours reading.

Time sped by quickly, and after two cups of coffee, it was already time for lunch. Hannah texted Anya, wondering if her best friend wanted to eat together like they usually did. She frowned when she read Anya's text back that she was busy this lunch break, so Hannah decided to grab a sandwich downstairs at the bistro again.

After purchasing the sandwich, Hannah found herself steering towards the skating rink again, wanting to see the budding young skaters. The dream had brought up the feelings of longing, prompting her to act on them.

She reached the rink quickly, and laid her crutches down onto the bench. She leaned forwards, towards the ice. Her eyes were attracted almost immediately by a young girl in a plain black leotard who was spinning around, having fun while her mother cheered her on. With her long brown hair tied back, it reminded Hannah of herself in her younger days.

She continued to watch the girl, mesmerized by the sight.

Suddenly, the little girl stumbled mid jump. She was just about to fall onto the ice when a man steadied her, smiling brightly. "Are you alright?" he asked her tenderly as he steadied her.

"Yes, thank you, sir!" She skated towards her worried mother, assuring the distressed woman that she was alright.

Gosh, I remember those days, Hannah thought. Skating used to make her mother really anxious. Her mother's eyes were always glued to Hannah, even though the cold was drying her pupils out, she could never truly relax when she took Hannah to practice. Hannah knew it and got up from every fall with a smile on her face, assuring her mother that she was totally fine – even if her butt did feel like it was on fire.

The man turned and his eyes caught on Hannah, still watching the exchange. She had a wonderful mesmerized look on her gorgeous face. Hannah noticed the man watching her, and realized that he looked familiar. The hair... the green eyes... Oh! It was the man from the coffee shop, a month ago!

Recognition hit as Hannah's surprised face turned into one of disgust. She remembered just how flirty he had been, and how she had found him a turnoff. She tore her eyes away from his face and instead focused on her sandwich, taking big, deliberate bites as she kept her eyes away from the rink.

But try as she might, she couldn't help but take a peek at his fantastic figure gliding around the rink. He slid on the ice like a natural, and was obviously very comfortable on the rink. His skates whooshed and slid as she forgot she was trying to not ogle him. Before she could stop herself, he had skated to a stop, right in front of her.

"Enjoying the show?" he asked with a grin, causing her to sneer.

"No, I'm just eating my sandwich," she retorted, taking a big bite just to prove her point.

"Why don't you join me on the ice instead?" he asked, not able to see her cast through the barrier of the rink's wall.

"No, thanks," she replied, deciding to not reveal that her leg was currently in a cast. "I don't want to."

A look of amusement came over the man's face. "Oh? And why not?"

"I just don't want to. And the sandwich doesn't want to either."

"Can you not skate?" he teased with a light smile. "Ah, that must be it, isn't it! C'mon, I'll teach you. I'll teach you how to jump and twirl, if you want."

Hannah had to hold back a smirk. "Maybe some other time."

He shrugged. "Suit yourself. I'm Andrew, by the way. And I'll be here all week." After flashing her one last brilliant smile, he pushed away from the side and started to skate again.

Hannah rolled her eyes as she sat back onto the bench, polishing off the rest of her sandwich. Oh, he was a looker alright, but not the type of man she liked at all. She thought back to Francis, the man she had thought was so honorable and loyal, who had betrayed her. Maybe she didn't have as good taste as she thought.

She checked her watch, realizing it was time to head back to work. She gave Andrew one last scathing look before getting up and propping herself back onto her crutches.

The last hours of work became torture. She found herself unable to concentrate fully on the documents she was supposed to be reading and checking over. Instead, all she could think about was skating.

All of a sudden, the chair she was sitting in was more boring than usual. The computer screen was putting her to sleep. All she wanted to do was to be back on the ice, gliding along like that little girl, practicing to her favorite music. But her leg was preventing her from that, and she was scared that even if she did get back on the ice, her leg wouldn't be strong enough to support her.

She thought about Andrew, and how he had tenderly helped the little girl. It was such a contrast to what she had assumed had been a typical player/flirt personality. She couldn't deny that she liked it, and was kind of intrigued that he liked to skate too. Maybe there was more to him than she had thought. And she would definitely like it if there was.

"Hey you, working hard or hardly working?"

Hannah was snapped out of her thoughts as she looked up, finding Anya right beside her with a big smile on her face. "Working very hard!" She laughed as Anya pulled back.

"Sure, sure, I believe you," Anya teased. "It's almost closing. Do you want to watch a movie tonight? I just bought a new tub of ice cream and some more packs of popcorn!"

"I'll only come if you don't make me watch horror movies again!" Hannah said as she swirled around in her chair to look at Anya, who was holding a hot cup of coffee in her hand. "How about a good old-fashioned romance?"

"Fine," Anya agreed before she took a sip. "Oh, and by the way, the higher-ups have told me that you've been doing a *fantastic* job. You know the Royce v. King case? Well, Royce won because of that discrepancy you caught! There might be a promotion in the works for you if you want to continue working here as a permanent paralegal!"

"Permanent?" Hannah repeated, rather stunned. "Really?"

"Well it's not official, *yet*. But I'm sure it will be soon." Anya grinned happily. "Okay, I just have to take care of one last thing before we go. I'll be back as soon as I can. Get ready to leave soon!"

"Okay, okay, got it. You're the boss!"

"I wish," Anya said with a wink. She stalked away, leaving Hannah alone with her thoughts again.

The rest of the night, Hannah was able to put her fears about the future away and she had a good time with her best friend. She had always been the type to stay at home instead of going out to a club, and was glad Anya shared the same sentiments.

The girls curled up on the couch, armed with an oversized fluffy blanket and plenty of snacks, and escaped into the haze of the whirlwind romance being played out on screen for them. Hannah's parents texted her just past midnight to ask how she was, and for the first time in a month her reply of *"I'm fine"* was not a lie.

The relaxing night was just what she needed, and when she went to sleep that night, it was with a wide smile on her face, thinking that though life threw her curveballs, it really was good. That night, she didn't have a single nightmare.

Chapter 7

The next day, Hannah woke up feeling refreshed.

She was excited to go to the rink during her break after stopping by the organic café, feeling more like her old self as she munched her free-range egg and mayo sandwich. It was good to be able to look forward to something related to skating... something she hadn't done in a while and was starting to feel further away from her reality. Just watching the skaters swish and swirl on that glowing stage was soothing to her, though she couldn't join in on the fun herself.

It suddenly made her realize just how much she had missed it. Well, actually, that was a lie. She knew how much she missed it. She just couldn't bear admitting that she couldn't live without it.

But work was keeping her busy, and was fulfilling. When she managed to catch mistakes or make contributions to the firm, her actions had positive results and she was becoming quite the popular lady among her workforce. She enjoyed working with Anya (how fun is it to work alongside your best friend in the whole world?), and had made many friends among her coworkers that she frequently hung out with after work. Plus, her bosses were seriously impressed with her, and seemed to forget that she had only six months of experience at law school.

Her routine stayed the same for the next month.

She worked, looking forward to the day she would be able to be back on the ice. She regularly went in for checkups with Dr. James, who had switched her hard cast to a walking one, allowing her to take away the crutches and walk normally. Well, as normally as she could with a giant black brace-like thing on her leg. He had even told her that she would be able to take off the walking cast soon too.

During her breaks, if she were alone, she would go down to the rink and watch the skaters. Today was no different.

Hannah stood in front of the rink, feeling as toasty as a Pop-Tart in her winter coat and scarf. The faux fur around the hood acted as a neck pillow and tickled a little bit, causing her to relax further. She noticed that Andrew was here today as he often was. Over the weeks they had exchanged many glances, but he hadn't come to talk to her again. It looked like today that all would be changed.

Andrew came to a stop in front of Hannah, smiling at her as his right boot's blade scraped the ice without making a sound.

Even his technique was cocky.

"Hey, you're here again."

"Yeah, I am," she replied dully as she played with a stray lock of her hair, pretending to look as uninterested as possible. "And so are you."

"Why're you always here? Yet you never skate yourself," he pondered as he leaned against the rail.

"I just like to watch. And you?"

"I skate in my free time, aka my lunches. It's my hobby, and keeps me in shape."

She didn't respond to this, as her attention was captured by a little boy practicing his jumps with precision. He fell hard, and her heart leaped in her chest, hoping he wasn't hurt. But the boy got up easily and flashed his mother a big smile before starting to skate again. It made her smile too, knowing he was okay. Skaters tended to look out for each other like that.

Andrew followed her gaze, also smiling when he watched the boy get up. "Perseverance. It's a wonderful thing."

Hannah nodded, turning her head to study Andrew, who was still watching the other skaters. He looked softer now, more handsome than he was sexy without the smirk on his face. She much preferred this look. Before she could turn away, he moved his head, and their eyes locked.

Quickly, she swung her head to the side, feeling her cheeks warm. "I-I'd better go, my lunch break is almost up."

"Alright. But before you do, you've never told me your name…" he said accusingly as he tilted his head. "I hope that's not by design."

"It's Hannah," she said before turning around and starting to walk away.

As Andrew pushed off the side onto the ice, he called out to her. "See you soon, Hannah."

***

Good news awaited Hannah on her trip to the hospital after work. She had been led to the examination room as usual by a nurse after x-rays, and was waiting for Dr. James to arrive. She hummed a tune to herself, one of the classical Mozart pieces she used to skate to, as she sat in a chair.

The door opened and Dr. James strolled in, looking tired in his scrubs and long white coat. "Hello, Hannah! Did you have to wait long?"

"No, no, it's fine!"

"That's good to hear. Let's see your x-rays." Several moments passed before he whirled around with a big smile on his face. "Great news, Hannah! Looks like during these past few months, your leg has been doing some quick healing!" Hannah smiled as the doctor's positive words washed over her. "Looks like all your training and practices have paid off. Having a healthy body is essential to healing well and at a good speed."

"So I will definitely be able to skate again?" she said eagerly, her face completely lit up with pure excitement. "And soon?"

"It's looking that way! We should be able to take the cast off soon, and you'll have to do some physical therapy to make sure that your functions return to normal, but other than that, everything will be alright."

That was exactly what Hannah had wanted to hear for so long. "Thank you so much, Dr. James! I'll do whatever it takes to make sure my leg heals properly."

"Okay, then you'll want to know this…" And he went on, Hannah listening intently, praying that nothing would go wrong and her leg would stay healed for good.

***

As she waited for her next appointment with Dr. James, the one where she would be getting her cast off, Hannah threw herself completely into leg care. She spent her time online researching ways to make sure her leg stayed fine, and to ensure that she didn't strain herself too much. She followed every single one of Dr. James' instructions, to the letter. The urge to put her skates back on was like an itch that she couldn't scratch, no matter how close she was to finding where the itch was.

The good thing was that she would have her cast off, very, very soon. She was so ready to be free from the restricting cast that she arrived to see Dr. James half an hour early. Jittery, Hannah sipped tea from her cute heart-shaped mug as she waited, wrapping her hands around the very warm sides of the mug, trying to heat up her digits.

The whole idea of having her cast completely off made her a little nervous, despite being excited for this moment for months. That was always the way — you wait so long for something and when you finally get it you don't understand why you were excited anymore. *I mean, I don't even have a coach anymore,* she kept thinking. It was going round and round her head like a negative mantra, or a strange nursery rhyme that was meant to scare her instead of sending her to sleep.

She hoped that the doctor wouldn't find an infection or something underneath the cast. Though she realized her fears were somewhat unfounded, the internet research she had done had freaked her out somewhat. She knew she should never trust Google!

"Hey, Hannah, ready to get that cast off?" Dr. James greeted her with a big smile.

She looked down at the big clunky thing on her leg, and returned his smile as she thought of what she could do without it. She could skate. She could get her life back (or some form of it, anyway). "Of course! Let's do this."

Chapter 8

The law firm kept Hannah busy with work for the next several weeks. As she sat at her desk, reading reports and attempting to decipher the legal jargon, she kept looking down at her leg, as though she kept forgetting that she had the cast off in the first place. But to be honest, she just liked looking at her newly freed leg, out of its solid prison and ready to step back on the ice as soon as she made good enough progress in therapy. She went to physical therapy several times each week, and was really feeling the difference. In fact, the physical therapist had told her that she was most likely able to skate, but to take it easy.

Even though she was able to, she was afraid.

What if she fell again? What if she was nowhere near the level she was before she broke her leg, and she just made a fool of herself on the ice?

Where was she going to get a new partner and trainer from?

Hannah didn't think she could handle being unable to skate. Yet the terror of hearing her bone shattering as it hit the ice still echoed in her mind.

But even with these fears in her mind, when she had finally completed enough paperwork to take a well-earned lunch break all to herself, Hannah found herself back at the ice rink. Though she tried to deny it to herself, to convince herself that she was only here to watch the budding skaters, she knew that a part of her was also looking for the smiling face of the graceful, handsome Andrew.

Her face fell a little when she realized that he wasn't on the ice. She was about to turn away to pick up a sandwich or a soup, when she bumped into something. "Oh!" Hannah exclaimed, flinging her hands up in surprise and immediately taking a few steps back.

"Whoa there," Andrew said, a huge smile blossoming on his face when he saw it was her.

"A-Andrew!" Hannah stuttered a little.

"Where are you headed?" The grin on his face never faded. He gazed down at her as he took a few steps back to give her some space.

"Lunch," Hannah replied, readjusting the strap of her bag and pointing to the exit, where she had just come through less than ten minutes earlier.

"You're not going to skate?" he asked. He held his black skating bag up. "Why don't you join me on the ice today?"

"No, I can't, my le..." Hannah trailed off when she looked down and remembered that she had her cast off. *Maybe I should try skating. It's been so long, after all.* Hannah pursed her lips.

"Your leg? There's nothing wrong with your leg!" Andrew smiled. "Come on, live a little! I told you before, I'll teach you how to skate!"

Hannah remembered she hadn't told him that she was a professional. Well, maybe it wouldn't be too bad to get back on the ice. "Okay, fine, teach me how to skate," she replied, a slightly amused look on her face.

Hannah followed Andrew to the rink, up to the skate rentals. "What size?" the bored-looking lady with frizzy red hair at the counter asked in a drawl.

"Seven," Hannah replied, wondering how anyone could be bored working at such an exciting place. The lady handed her a pair of white skates, and when Hannah put on the pair of pure white shoes, a familiar feeling came over her. God, it felt so good to put on the figure skates again. She did up the laces in double-quick time and checked over the blades to make sure they weren't damaged.

"You certainly look like you've done that a lot before," Andrew commented as he pulled on his own black shoes.

Hannah said nothing, wondering how he was going to teach her. It would be fun to play along, she mused.

"Let's go," he prompted, offering her his hand. She took it, feeling a bit of a strange dip in her stomach as they touched properly for the first time, and followed him onto the rink.

Her first steps were hesitant, as if it were truly her first time on the ice. She was afraid of her leg giving out on her, though it had already healed. The pain and the horror from the fall still slightly echoed in her mind, and it showed clearly in her footsteps as she took one tiny step after the other on the pure white rink. But *oh my God,* it felt so good to step foot on ice again. It was comparable to a bird getting its wings back.

"It's okay," Andrew goaded. "I won't let you fall."

It was weird, but those plain words made her feel so safe; so protected. A part of her believed that yes, he wouldn't let her fall, which was odd since they hadn't known each other for very long. "Okay," she replied, her innocent face gazing up at the guy who she didn't know all that well yet trusted alarmingly quickly.

Testing the waters, she pushed forward, gliding on her skates. God, it felt good. The feelings she had not felt for so long on the ice came rushing back to her, putting a brilliant smile on her face, and allowing her to fully relax into her legs and feet so she had better flow in her skating.

Andrew watched her with something akin to amazement, as he could almost literally see a change coming over her. She had previously seemed shy and quiet, but when she was on the ice… He thought it was absolutely beautiful, the way her face lit up. But he wondered why such a change came over her. Wasn't she supposed to be a new skater?

Hannah temporarily forgot that Andrew was even there as she began to take bigger strides, the wind rushing through her hair, sending it spiraling backwards as though it was trying to join in with the dancing. He simply stopped and stared for a moment, before realizing that he should probably catch up to her and make good on his promise to not allow her to fall.

Andrew sped after her, mesmerized by the way Hannah seemed to simply glide on the ice. She looked absolutely breathtaking, and completely at home. When she finally slowed down, and he was able to catch up to her, he stared at her, bewildered. "Hannah!" he started, pretending to be insulted. "You lied to me!"

"Huh?" Hannah replied, a smile creeping up on her lips and dying to break free. "When did I?"

"You told me you couldn't skate!"

Hannah smirked. "When did I say that?" Her leg was feeling strong, and she was feeling an overwhelming rush of emotion as she had thought she would never be able to feel this wind ever again.

"You said it whe—" Andrew trailed off as he reflected on their conversations, and remembered that it was he who had assumed that she wasn't able to skate. "Oh!"

"Remember now?" Hannah laughed. Being on the ice always put her in such a good mood, one that Andrew noticed.

"Oops," he said sheepishly, laughing along with her. Her melodic giggling was truly contagious, and he couldn't help but smile along. He couldn't tear his eyes away from her, watching her as their skates scraped on the ice.

In a split second, Hannah's happy smile turned into a look of surprise. "Look out!" Hannah exclaimed, making a rushed grab towards him. Hannah's hand found his jacket and she gave it a hard tug, pulling him away. Andrew had been skating while watching her, and had almost crashed straight into the wall!

But the sudden imbalance of weight sent Andrew propelling towards Hannah, and before she could skate away, he had knocked her down. Hannah hit the ice, but thankfully hit it at the angle that made for the minimum of damage. "Ouch," Hannah exclaimed, rubbing her back as she pushed herself up.

Andrew had fallen along with her, and their legs tangled in a heap as they stared at each other. They held each other's gaze for a split second before hurriedly breaking it to pull their legs away. A slow blush grew on Hannah's face, giving her pale cheeks some color. "Sorry about that," Andrew murmured.

"Watch where you're going!" Hannah exclaimed, with no anger behind the words. She brushed her hands across her leg, breathing a sigh of relief after realizing that it was alright. She was stronger than she thought. "At least you didn't crash into the wall."

"I got injured anyways," Andrew laughed. "But thanks for pulling me away."

"I tried!" Hannah retorted, slowly pushing herself to her feet and being careful not to put too much pressure on her leg. She found herself liking the way he laughed... the way his entire face lit up with an unexplainable sort of happiness. It was so carefree, and drew her in like a magnet. Blinking, Hannah realized she had been intently staring at him as he straightened back up. She hoped he hadn't noticed her gaze.

"Like what you see?" he asked with something akin to a cross between a smile and a smirk, shattering all faith she had that he hadn't seen.

"Not at all," she said, giggling before she pushed off with one foot, starting to skate across the ice again.

Suddenly, music poured over the loudspeakers, and Hannah recognized it instantly. *Mozart.*

It was as if the people around her faded away, and she were taken over by some sort of spirit. A new spring came into Hannah's movements, and before she could stop herself, she was gliding around the ice doing crossovers, lifting her leg high, and switching to backwards skating. This continued for the entire song, and when it ended, Hannah seemed to come back into herself.

"Phew!" She exhaled a breath of air as she stood on the ice, feeling very confident after she had fully "performed" the step bit of the routine. She felt absolutely exhilarated, and it was an addicting feeling.

"Okay, seriously, how often do you skate? That was absolutely amazing!" Andrew sped beside her, his eyes wide open in surprise. He had been practicing for a long time himself during lunch times, but felt that he was nowhere near the level she was and with such ease! "You must have trained somewhere before?"

Knowing the gig was up, Hannah decided she might as well let Andrew know the truth. "Alright, fine, I concede. I actually used to be a professional figure skater. And when I say used to be, I mean that I stopped a few months ago."

"Oh wow! That explains it." Andrew exclaimed. "Wait, so why don't you skate anymore?" From what he had seen of her, she seemed perfectly fine where her technique was concerned, and his curiosity was burning. Going purely by the look on her face when she was on the ice, she seemed to really enjoy being on the ice.

"I… I broke my leg. Really badly," she said, wincing as she remembered how painful the break had been for her.

Andrew's face turned somber as he looked at her. "I'm so sorry. That must have been terrible…" There was a tension in the air now, and Andrew wracked his brain for something he could say that would relieve it. Just as he was about to speak, Hannah's stomach rumbled. "Hungry?" he asked, letting out a small laugh, remembering that he had pulled her away from getting her lunch to join him in the rink.

"A little," Hannah replied, rubbing at her stomach. It growled again. "Okay, a lot!"

"Why don't you grab some lunch with me?" Andrew said seriously. "My treat."

Hannah thought about it for a split second. "Alright." She smiled, thinking what harm could one lunch do?

The two headed off of the ice, and soon were walking towards a nearby café. "So what do you do,

Andrew?" she asked. His button-up shirt and tie weren't fantastic indicators of what he did.

"Ah, just some boring business job. I'd tell you more, but you'd be bored to tears. Tell me more about skating!"

Hannah recounted to him how she had first started skating, and how Francis and Erica had left her while she was in her hospital bed. By the time they had reached the café, he felt as if he had learned quite a bit about her. "That Francis guy sounds like a real tool," he sympathized. "It's a miracle that your leg healed so nicely, though! How does it feel?"

"A lot better now, thank you." She walked through the door that he held open for her. They were seated quickly, and before long, Andrew had Hannah forgetting all about Francis as they chatted about all sorts of things. Hannah found that Andrew really was quite friendly, and somehow managed to make her laugh with all his interesting jokes and anecdotes.

Just as Andrew launched into a tale about his work acquaintance's rowdy dog, Hannah's phone rang. "Sorry," she said as she read the text that had come in. *Hannah, are you almost back yet?* it read, and Hannah winced. "I'm going to be late!" she yelped, standing up from the table hurriedly.

"Oh, you'd better hurry. I'll take of things here." Andrew stood up too. Just as Hannah turned to leave, he caught her by the arm. "Wait, just a moment." His eyes resembled those of a puppy dog. He was practically melting at the sight of her. "Can I have your number?" He handed his phone to her, and she decided that yes, she'd definitely like to see him again, so she gave him her real number.

Hannah gave him his phone back before almost sprinting out the door, in a hurry to return to the firm. Andrew watched her leave, never taking his eyes off her, all the while thinking that she was quite an interesting girl.

Chapter 9

Hannah was practically breaking a sweat by the time she got back to the law firm — she couldn't run too much on her leg and so she was late. Fifteen minutes to be exact.

Anya hurried up to Hannah when she walked through the door, her eyes bulging out of their sockets and shushing Hannah to her desk.

"Oh my God! Quickly, get back to your desk. No one can see that you're late." Still slightly out of breath from power walking back to work, Hannah spoke. "I just got held up at the ice rink... I went back on the ice for the first time!"

Anya looked slightly unimpressed. "I'm happy for you and all, but you can't be late to this job! They take things like that really seriously. Plus it makes me look bad because I was the one that recommended they hire you!"

Less calm now about the situation, Hannah replied, "Just the once won't hurt though?"

An exasperated Anya rolled her eyes. "Yeah it will, Han! If you do it again you get a formal warning, and if you keep doing it, then you won't have a job anymore."

"I'm so sorry, An. I promise it won't happen again."

Anya gave her a quick hug. "I hate to be strict, but you don't want to lose this job. It's good for you, and until you get a new trainer you may as well stay here and earn some money."

Anya was right. She was always right.

"Now I've got to get back to work myself. I'll see you afterwards though? You can tell me all about your first day back on the ice!"

And with that, Hannah was left to her paperwork and her thoughts. Only she didn't get any paperwork done that afternoon, because she was too busy gushing over Andrew and the newfound respect she had for him. Or maybe it wasn't just respect. Maybe it was something more.

***

The next few weeks were a bit of a whirlwind for Hannah. Her days consisted of following the same routine: she would shower in the morning, get a ride to work with Anya, break for lunch and go to the rink to see Andrew, go back to work, and then finish work and skip the ride home with Anya to train at the rink with Andrew until late into the night.

Even after her training was over (sometimes they didn't stop skating until almost eleven o'clock) Andrew would insist on getting something to eat at a restaurant or a bar. She just couldn't say no to him, though it wasn't for lack of trying.

"So, you wanna go grab some dinner? I know this great little place downtown, not too far from here, and not that many people know about it so it will be like a secret hideaway from the outside world."

His suggestions often sounded rather romantic, she thought, but he hadn't made any advances or shown that he was even remotely interested, so Hannah didn't care to ponder upon the idea of a candlelit dinner if perfectly good candles were going to be wasted.

"I can't tonight, Andrew, I promised to give Anya a call when I got home. We had a lot of work to do and she just wanted to run past this form with me."

He never looked hurt, just shocked that Hannah would dare choose anyone else over him. Like he was meant to be her priority!

"Aw no, Han, don't do this to me. I've booked the table already!" he said dramatically. He even started to produce tears that didn't fall but made his eyes all glossy, making it harder for Hannah to tear away (they were nice eyes, after all) and twice as hard for her to say no to someone who looked like it was your fault their world was crashing down around them, even though she knew it was fake.

"I really shouldn't... if we don't fill in the form we'll be behind tomorrow..."

"I sense a 'but' coming on."

"No, I should really go home."

He took her hand and used his thumb to massage it, sending little shivers down her spine and making her forget about the stupid forms.

"Come on… just this once?"

"You say that every day!"

"Well, this time I mean it."

"No you don't!"

"Fine then, I don't. But if you want me to listen to you in training then you better come with me."

Hannah gasped jokingly. "Is that some kind of twisted blackmail? Do you want to restore power to men, is that it? Are you a misogynist?"

"Yes, it is blackmail. And no, it is only right that you have all of the power. An ice king is nothing without his ice queen, after all."

And then she would give in and go to dinner, forgetting about her responsibilities until she got home and had seven missed calls from Anya or her parents or whoever else Andrew caused her to avoid.

She didn't know what it was about him, but although she would always try to decline, she secretly wished every time that he wouldn't take no for an answer. She wished that he would keep asking, keep his interest in her, and keep booking tables for underground restaurants that only a handful of people knew about. They were just good friends, who liked spending time together and engaging in flirty behavior with each other.

Yes… they were just good friends.

Hannah made a promise to herself one night that she would stop obsessing about Andrew and not make a move before he did. She refused to let herself get the wrong idea until it was proved that Andrew liked her as more than a friend. Besides, she needed to focus on getting back to her usual skating standard and trying to improve to a professional level while also teaching Andrew, who had only ever skated as a hobby.

Well, that was her plan.

Until this happened.

It was a Sunday night, a month or so after Hannah's cast had been taken off, and both Hannah and Andrew had the day off work. They had been on the rink practically all day, only stopping to rest, drink water, and eat some light snacks. It was coming up to eight o'clock in the evening and there was just one more thing that Hannah wanted to show Andrew before they stepped off the ice.

"We're nearly done for today, but I want to show you something first."

Andrew was confused. "What do you want to show me?"

"Step back and you'll see."

Andrew did as he was told, and skated back to the wall of the rink, where he used his hands to push up onto the higher surface and sit down so he could get a view of what Hannah wanted to show him.

He wasn't prepared for what he saw.

Hannah skated back to the music player and hooked her phone into the system, scanning her special playlist for the song she needed. She hadn't told him, but she had been coming to the rink and practicing a routine before even going to work during the morning.

Pressing play on the music, she took her position in the center of the rink.

"Yesterday" by the Beatles started to echo out onto the rink. Hannah got into character, and wore a distant and chilling expression on her face.

Andrew's breath caught in his throat as Hannah pushed away from her starting position.

Yesterday, all my troubles seemed so far away... She waltz jumped, gliding along and turning around so she was looking behind her shoulder, and spun before taking off into the air and landing with her left foot in the air, making sure to keep moving in this position for a few seconds.

Suddenly, I'm not half the man I used to be, there's a shadow hanging over me... a pained look on her face as she slowed for a moment to look gracefully from left to right, as if searching for the shadow or the other half of herself. Immediately picking up the speed again, she moved into a layback spin, arching her back backwards and bringing her arms over her head, almost like she had just woken up and was doing a stretch to warm up her bones.

Meanwhile, Andrew was completely entranced. It seemed like everything Hannah had wanted to say about her accident, but was too afraid to, was trapped inside the lyrics of the song and the meaning she gave to the dance. He decided in that moment that there was nothing more beautiful than the sight of this girl opening up her soul to him. He wanted to watch her forever.

Why she had to go? I don't know, she wouldn't say, I said something wrong, now I long for yesterday... coming to the end of the song, Hannah picked up speed one last time and went for the big move – a camel spin changing quickly into a donut spin, and rising back up while still spinning to perform the Biellmann spin, grabbing one of the blades on her skates and pulling her leg up over her head. Her sleek ponytail danced along with her to the same beat, giving the routine an added feeling of completeness. To end, she covered her face with her hands as if she was crying, and laid her head to one side of her neck.

The music stopped, and silence fell on the rink.

Andrew wasn't clapping. Or cheering. Or saying anything.

He was so incredibly shocked. He said nothing for a moment and then broke into a glorious smile.

"You really don't know how good you are, do you?"

Hannah was taken aback by this comment. "Uh... I mean it's been a while since I put together an entire routine and performed it for an audience—"

"You're amazing. Absolutely amazing." Andrew grinned. "You want to go get something to eat?"

"Okay. But haven't we been to just about every place that serves food in the county?"

Andrew jumped off the wall and looked back at her as he stepped off the ice. "Trust me; you won't have been here before."

***

He was right; she had never been there before.

Because *there* was the roof of a building near the ice rink.

Hannah was a bit confused, but decided to go along with it anyway.

"I'm confused."

But the more she looked, the more she noticed that this wasn't quite the random dinner invitation that she first thought it was. The perimeter of the roof was laced in dainty fairy lights that lit up the pathway to the picnic blanket and the pile of cushions that awaited her. The moon shone down and smiled at the skaters, while making itself useful as a spotlight for the basket of food that lay near the blanket.

"It was meant to be a thank-you for teaching me so well these past few weeks," Andrew said cautiously, as though he didn't want to stir Hannah from her thoughts. Either that or he was scared the exposure to the moonlight would make her angry, and she might turn into a werewolf that would devour him for assuming she would be interested in such a date-like setting. "Now it's more a sign of appreciation for skating like that for me."

Still in a minor state of shock, Hannah spoke up. "Skating is just what I do… I was just showing you what level you could be at too in the future."

"Skating isn't just what you do, and you know it. Skating is in your blood. Not everyone who skates can move like you can, while moving other people. You're special."

Hannah's cheeks reddened at the compliment, while Andrew led the way and sat down on the blanket, arranging a few pillows around him and breathing in the mild night air. She gingerly walked over and sat

81

beside him, relaxing onto the fluffy blanket and laying her head on one of the cushions.

"I thought I was okay. A few silly mistakes but nothing that can't be fixed relatively quickly." She let the silence fill the spaces while she paused to think. "Francis never gave me a compliment like that before."

Moving the picnic basket closer towards them, getting out some chips, dip, and iced tea, he responded, "It's a good thing you're not his partner anymore, then, because he sounds like an idiot."

Hannah sat up to take a mason jar of iced tea. "He isn't an idiot, actually. He's wise beyond his years, especially when it comes to skating."

Andrew leaned closer to Hannah in order to reach the chips, and looked directly into her eyes, his own glistening with wit and beauty. "Anyone who doesn't think you are amazing is an idiot in my eyes."

And with that, she was looking back at him and the silence fell back down, leaving an intangible force of electricity flying around them.

A few caught breaths later and their hands were interlocked, noses and foreheads touching, and eyelids batting on smiling faces.

"You're cool," Hannah whispered.

Andrew smirked. "Ice cool?"

Hannah immediately pulled away and rolled onto the blanket, giggling. "Oh my God! You just ruined a perfectly romantic moment with your skating jokes!"

Andrew turned to look down at Hannah, whose body was now shaking slightly from all of the laughing she was doing. He found it impossible not to join in.

"No! The moment isn't ruined... it was just an icebreaker!"

Now both of them were in fits of laughter and forgot all about the moonlight and the fairy lights and the picnic food. They were glad to have each other in that moment.

When the laughing had subsided a bit, they were both lying on their sides on the blankets, facing each other.

"I mean it, though," Hannah said. "You're cooler than I thought you were when I first saw you in the café."

Andrew pretended to be offended. "What did you think of me when you first met me?"

"Oh you know – a show-off. And pretentious."

"Oh, well now I know where I stand."

In that second, Hannah leaned in and brought her lips to Andrew's, bringing her hand to his chest and pulling him closer by his shirt.

When she let him go, she said only one thing. "That's where. And technically, you're sitting down."

They both laughed, and spent the rest of the night talking, kissing, and dancing on the roof. When the moon said goodbye and allowed the sun to take its place, they were so tired, so warm wrapped in the blanket that they fell asleep. However, they were in for a rude awakening.

The two were woken by the gut-wrenching sound of Hannah's alarm on her smartphone to signal it was time for work.

"Oh God, I've got to go."

"No you don't."

"But work!"

"You really want to leave now? When everything is perfect? Hannah, you have spent your life working for people who don't appreciate you. Spend some more time with the person who does."

And it was those words only that persuaded her to stay, allowing herself to live in the moment, and forget about everything but skating and Andrew.

Chapter 10

She may have allowed herself to live in the moment, but the moment she got into work was not a pleasant one.

She was two hours late.

And Anya wasn't even there to save her. Instead, the deputy manager of the firm came up to her desk as a slightly sweaty Hannah panted over to her desk and rushed to set up her computer before they got to her.

Ms. Walters, the deputy manager, was a round-looking woman with tortoise-shell rimmed glasses. She spoke with an unusual air of affluence. Eying Hannah at her desk, she marched over and leaned over her.

"Miss Avery, may I ask why you were so late to work this morning?"

Holy crap, this is it, thought Hannah. *I'm so going to get fired!*

"Um... I... I... slept past my alarm. I promise it won't happen again."

Ms. Walters grinned — well, it was more of a snarl, really — and placed her hands on the top of Hannah's desk as if to show her who was boss.

"Oh that's okay, Hannah, I know it won't happen again. You'll be fired before you even have the chance to get through the door and pretend you're working on your computer." She pointed to the blackened screen that Hannah had been pretending to use for the thirty seconds before she came over. "I don't know what you're up to, young lady, but I am going to inform the manager about this incident and let him decide whether you stay on in the future."

So Hannah was saved for that day, at least.

Two of her co-workers, Bernice and Neil, considerably older than her but with ears like two hawks, turned around from their desks and gave her a sympathetic look.

"Don't worry, Hannah, it is all an empty threat. They would be getting rid of a valuable member of the team if they fired you. They won't want to lose you," said Bernice.

"Oh I don't know," retorted Neil. "She's only been here for a couple of months. Besides, everyone is replaceable."

Don't I know it, Hannah thought, recalling the day that Francis ditched her for his new pretty-faced partner.

"You'll be fine! It's never going to happen again. You must have got a really good reason for being so late today – smart girls like you don't just turn up late because you missed the alarm. Did you have another health scare on the ice last night?" asked Bernice.

"Something like that, yes." Hannah said no more on the matter, and they all got back to work. *If only they knew I ditched work for a boy.* Since when did Hannah become that type of silly love-struck girl that ditches her responsibilities?

***

Andrew called her once she had finished work. Ten whole minutes after, to be precise.

"Are you coming into the rink today? We've got a lot to work on if you want me as good as you were last night."

Feeling a bit... there was no other word for it but annoyed, with Andrew, she took quite a sharp tone on the phone. "You know I'll be there, I always am."

"Whoa, Miss Cranky Pants, what has gotten into you? I thought you had a great time last night."

She had. Oh God, she really had. The second best thing to skating was getting to fraternize with her partner. If Erica could see her now, she would be mortified. Part of the reason why she couldn't even ask Francis out was because Erica thought that once partners became *partners*, in real life, all of the chemistry vanished on the ice. So, it was imperative that they keep their relationship professional. Plus, with Erica repeating that phrase over and over again, there was no way Francis was going to attempt asking Hannah out – especially if it meant ruining his career.

"Sorry, I'm just tired. I'll be over soon, please say you have some of the picnic left over from last night? I feel like I need to comfort-eat right now."

"I've got the remains of our feast, yes! I was kind of hoping to save them for after rehearsal though?"

"No, no, I'm eating them as soon as I get through the door and that's decided. If you want some I suggest you save a portion now, and then stand away from me. I'm so hungry from stress I feel like I would eat you if it meant forgetting about my woes."

Andrew guffawed and in that confident tone replied, "You're so funny, Han. See ya soon."

"Yeah, see you soon."

Sighing, she put down the phone. Still being no closer to getting another coach, on the verge of losing her job, and having to deal with a somewhat clingy friend-who-is-a-boy or whatever the hell he was, Hannah was certainly not in the mood to do anything other than climb into bed and hibernate there until summer.

When she got to the rink, Andrew was there waiting for her, a big grin on his face. He looked like he had just found out he'd won the lottery.

"You ready to start?"

Hannah sat down on the bench to put on her skates, tying the laces as slowly as possible. "I need to talk to you first."

The smile vanished from Andrew's face and he jumped off the ice, taking his place next to her on the stiff wooden bench.

"Okay…"

Hannah sighed. "I think we need to talk."

"That is pretty much the most overused sentence," he said, trying to keep the mood light, but a rising feeling of dread pooling in his stomach.

Trying not to make eye contact, she surreptitiously shifted away from him on the bench and fumbled with her laces some more.

"About last night, I–"

"I knew you didn't like it. You could have just told me!" Andrew said, trying not to raise his voice.

"No! Please don't get that idea. I really liked it, honestly. It was unexpected in a really nice way."

The smile returned to Andrew's face, a bit smaller this time.

"It's just that you're kind of making me put you first… which means I don't get that much sleep when I get home… and then I'm late for work the next day…"

"So you want to stop skating with me? Is that it?" Andrew's brow furrowed.

"No! Gosh, let me speak, will you? I just mean that I can't be having these crazy late-night restaurant adventures with you as often. Skating is my priority, but my job is also kind of high up on the list right now. I can't lose it. I might not have any other options but to work there for the rest of my life!"

Andrew scooted closer to Hannah on the bench and his tone of voice put her at ease. "I'm so sorry, Hannah. I had no idea how much it was all getting to you... how much I was getting to you. I promise I'll think before I plan any more restaurant trips."

"Thank you."

"And if I'm overwhelming you, please tell me. I never want you to feel uncomfortable to say no with me."

A gush of admiration came over Hannah and she rested her head on Andrew's shoulder, not without planting a kiss on his cheek first.

"Can we skate now?" she whispered into his jacket.

He let out a small laugh and placed his head on top of hers. "Of course." Then he slipped out of the position and waddled onto the ice with his skates. "The last one to complete ten laps around the rink is a loser!"

Feeling so much better about the situation after that talk, Hannah couldn't help smiling and getting up to join him. *He's not so bad,* she decided. *Not so bad at all.*

***

A couple more weeks passed, and everything was going well. Andrew had not kept her late after practice, he was improving massively, and she had not had any more warnings from the law firm.

Until one day, when Hannah had finished work, a familiar figure was outside to greet her at the door.

"Andrew, how did you know where the law firm was?"

"I looked it up!"

"But I'm on my way over to the rink now, like I do every day straight after work. Why are you here?"

Andrew cleared his throat and held out his hand, which Hannah resisted to take until she knew what was going on. "I cordially invite you to join me for some dinner, Miss Avery."

Though she found the posh accent he used to ask her out hilarious, she wasn't going to give him the satisfaction of feeling proud of his idea. "I thought I'd told you no more dinner dates!"

"Well, I thought since it had been a couple of weeks since we last went out, that maybe it had been enough time and you wouldn't be as angry at me for taking you somewhere?"

"You've already booked the reservations, haven't you?"

Andrew pursed his lips like a guilty child. "Maybe?"

Hannah freaked out. "Oh my God!"

"Don't stress! I'm going to treat you tonight, as an extra special thank-you for working so hard to teach me more advanced stuff on the ice."

"And what about practice today?"

"We'll blow it off!" He cupped her red cheeks (partly from the cold, partly from being angry with Andrew) with both of his hands. "You need a break. Plus, didn't you say I'd just about mastered the death spiral!"

That is true, Hannah thought. "Okay, I suppose one night can't hurt. Where were you thinking of going?"

"You'll see." And with that, he took her hand and started running and pulling her along with him.

Chapter 11

Andrew led her up to the door of a mysterious building. Through the windows she could see chandeliers bouncing light onto each and every person's face, and flickering candles on tables along with the flames from a roaring fire in a fireplace. The restaurant was decorated like a cross between a palace in the countryside and a wooden chalet on the snow-covered mountains of France where couples usually go for skiing vacations.

And as the security man took Andrew's name at the door, they were greeted inside the cozy building with a warm smile from all of the waiters, which gave Hannah goose bumps on her arms in the most comforting way. It relaxed her to know that they were welcome here.

"I know the head chef here," Andrew said. "He'll let us order anything and everything for free. No charge, we just sit and enjoy the meal and the atmosphere."

"Whoa, really?"

"Of course! This is your chance to be looked after by me for a change. I feel like you're always the one helping me out – picking me up from falls when I get so tired I can't get back up, being patient with the many mistakes I have made, and always being there to talk to me if I feel overwhelmed. I owe this to you."

They were taken to their table by a friendly face in a bow tie and they had pride of place at the biggest window in the restaurant, slightly further away from the hustle and bustle of the other tables.

"Would you like a menu, sir? And one for your lovely young lady too?"

"Of course, Michael, I always love to hear what new dishes Sal is preparing."

"I will be over in one moment with your menus and a list of today's specials."

"Thank you, Michael. I appreciate it."

"Oh, and don't forget, Andrew, tonight the restaurant is open until the early hours of the morning, which means that a night of piano music and taking to the dance floor is required!"

"Perfect."

"NO! NOT PERFECT NOT PERFECT NOT PERFECT!"

Hannah woke up hyperventilating, because she knew that wasn't a dream. That was simply a recall of what had happened last night. Or did she mean this morning?

Unfortunately for Hannah, it wasn't even still the morning. A record-breaking three and a half hours late, she could either not show up for work at all and chicken out of facing her consequences, or take her punishment the brave way.

As Hannah rushed to get ready, she couldn't help but let her thoughts drift back to last night.

"Come on, dance with me!"

The grand piano in the corner of the room was tinkling a beautiful melodic tune. She didn't recognize the name of the songs that were playing, but they were all songs that you could easily skate to. Hannah and Andrew had already eaten three courses of food and retired to a private lounge in another room for an hour to let their food digest. That room alone was beautiful, with thick gingham-patterned armchairs and another fireplace. There wasn't anyone else in there, and so they could put their feet up and enjoy the silence.

Hannah and Andrew could have talked about the next skating jump they were going to try out the next day, but instead decided to breathe in the quiet and lean back on the chairs, moving only to hold each other's hands. Hannah found that she didn't have to talk all the time when she was with Andrew. And he didn't have any dire need to talk about skating all the time, like Francis did. If it was Francis who had taken her out to dinner, he would have thrown the chairs out of the window if it meant clearing a space for them to practice routines for an extra hour that day. He always used to say that time was of the essence, and so you should never waste time by doing nothing.

What person denies another person some relaxation time? That was part of the reason why Hannah had taken such a liking to Andrew. He cared about spending time with her — not about spending time with her skating abilities.

Then they were escorted back into the main restaurant area where they were given a sorbet to cleanse their palate, and the piano was joined by a double bass, a trumpet, and a trombone. The music's genre changed to jazz and other restaurant goers were taking to the dance floor, and she felt the dancing buzz.

Once Hannah and Andrew were on that dance floor, they took center stage, and applied all of their paired twists and turns that they would normally do on the ice to the wooden surface. The other people at the restaurant could not keep their eyes off them, and it felt amazing. Performing for an audience gave her such a massive sense of achievement.

Above all of the music, and while still moving in time to the rhythm, she leaned close to Andrew's ear and tried to shout over the noise. "I've been thinking. I think you're ready to dance in front of people professionally. Why don't we sign up to the U.S. Championships?"

Andrew looked at her for a moment before drawing her in for a long and passionate kiss, lips just grazing each other and noses bumping cutely. When he retreated, he said one thing only.

"Let's do it."

Hannah couldn't get dressed quickly enough. There was no time for breakfast, brunch, lunch... she knew she wouldn't be long in the law firm today anyway. Just enough time for her to pack her things and leave.

The inevitable happened when she finally arrived. All of her co-workers stared at her, fear in their eyes, especially for her. The boss had gotten their assistant to leave a Post-it note on her desk, saying, "My office, as soon as you bother to show up."

And with that she was officially released from her job. The law firm job that Anya had been so kind to get her into, and now she had ruined the chance of having a stable career if figure skating didn't work out.

Anya wasn't pleased either. As Hannah was putting her things that cluttered her desk into a cardboard box, Anya came around the corner.

"How the hell did you manage to get fired?" she said, trying to keep her voice low but it wasn't really working. "Do you know how tough it was for me to get you this job in the first place? And this is how you repay me? By staying out late with that idiotic boyfriend of yours and not bothering to come to work because you're so busy being in love with him?"

Hannah was shocked that these words were even coming out of Anya's mouth. All of the employees sat silently around them, eavesdropping into the drama that was unfolding before their eyes.

"He's not my boyfriend! And for your information, I did care about this job! But do you know what I care about more? Figure skating. This job was only meant to be temporary anyway!" Hannah was hurt, and her words reflected it.

"Temporary! I only said that because I wanted you to give it a try, and I prayed that you'd like it enough to stay because you can't keep kidding yourself with this crazy dream that you're going to be a world-famous skater!" Anya exclaimed, before immediately covering her mouth with her hands and retreating backwards, regretting her words.

Hannah stood with her fists balled up and angry tears threatening to break loose. "What?"

"Hannah, I'm sorry. Things just got a bit out of hand. I didn't mean it!"

"Of course you meant it! Some friend you are," Hannah snapped, picking up her box of possessions and striding over to the door. "I'm off to the ice rink now to do what I'm meant to do — skating. Don't bother calling tonight, because I'll be training late. That's what professionals do."

And with that she walked out of the door, leaving mouths wide open and her best friend behind her.

***

It had been a few days since she got fired, and getting up in the morning was becoming an increasingly difficult task. She had lost her job, her best friend, and her dignity. Anya hadn't called her, and she was mad at Andrew, who got the brunt of her anger when she shouted at him during practice.

"Andrew! Straighten your back and get that left leg at a ninety-degree angle like the real skaters do it!"

"I am a real skater! I've got skates on, haven't I?"

"Shut up, and stop disrespecting me like that! Straighten that leg and then you'll be a real skater."

There was some kind of internal weight holding her down, where the heart was meant to be. It stopped the muscles on her face from smiling and stopped her brain from filtering mean words. Her life was even worse than while she was in the hospital.

Just as she was about to clamp her eyes shut again and go to sleep, her phone rang.

"Who's that?" she said to nobody. No one wanted to speak to her, so who was calling her? She picked up her phone anyway and prepared for some kind of argument. "Hello? Who's calling?"

A familiar voice greeted her at the other end of the phone. "Hannah? It's Erica."

Erica Summers. "Hi, Erica."

"I heard your leg was feeling better!"

Something was weird about this. "Yes, it's fine, thanks. In fact, I've improved my skating a lot."

Erica gave a small cough. "Well, that's what I wanted to talk to you about. I'd heard that your skating has vastly improved despite your accident. I wonder if you want to come back and skate for me again."

So that was why she was calling.

There were two sides to this situation. On the one hand, Hannah could be getting the proper training with the best woman in the business. On the other hand, she would be signing a deal with the devil — well — the woman who abandoned her because she was no longer useful to her.

But a second chance was being handed to her on a plate. Her pride could not play a part in this decision.

"I'll come back... But I'd like to bring my own partner, Andrew." That was Hannah's one condition. She wasn't going to sell out completely.

"Who is Andrew?"

"This guy that I've been training with. He is a great skater and a perfect partner for me."

"Oh! How long has he been professional for?"

That was the only problem. "He's not a pro, actually. He's a guy that I met at the rink, but we want to enter the U.S. Championships together."

"An amateur! I can't deal with amateurs, Hannah, and you know it. We'll find you another partner when you get back to your home turf."

Hannah was not backing down. "I'm not coming back unless Andrew comes back with me."

There were a few seconds of silence before Erica gave in. "Okay. He gets one chance to show me what he can do on the ice. If I decide I can't train him, he goes. Got it?"

"Got it."

"I'll see you this afternoon, honey. Welcome back on the team!"

"See you later!" And they mutually hung up the phone.

Breathing a huge sigh of relief, Hannah felt some of the heavy weight lifted immediately. Her phone pinged with the notification of a text, just minutes after she had spoken to Erica.

"Congratulations on going pro again. Love you loads.—A"

Anya! So it was she who called Erica and persuaded her to put Hannah back on the professional team. Now she knew where Erica had heard that she had improved so much. Hannah had thought it was strange that Erica called her out of the blue.

God, she felt so guilty for saying all those mean things to Anya, and immediately texted Anya back saying how sorry she was, and how much she regretted their fight.

It seemed like in the space of a morning, she had got both her trainer and her best friend back. Things were looking up.

When Andrew and Hannah got to her old rink that afternoon, Erica had no problem with Andrew's skating abilities.

"That was a good arabesque and Y-spin, Han," Erica muttered to her from the sidelines as Andrew performed a freestyle program on the ice. "You've taught him well."

"Thanks," beamed Hannah, "he's got exceptional balance. His hold-and-line while he's doing it is just as good as Francis."

"As good as Francis!" Erica said. "Honey, put him up against Francis at the moment and he'll destroy him. Francis is really struggling without you."

Hannah turned her head quickly from looking at Andrew to Erica. "Seriously?"

"Yeah! Don't get me wrong, you know what Francis is like – a perfectionist. He's beautiful. But his partner doesn't complement him like you used to."

This was surprising news to Hannah. Surprising, but not devastating. "So, you think Andrew and I can compete in the U.S. Championships as a pair?"

Erica smiled. "Oh, definitely! There's nothing stopping you!"

Andrew's music stopped and both Erica and Hannah clapped, their noise filling up the otherwise empty ice rink. He started gliding towards the sideline and

Hannah was smiling at him in admiration, before she felt a presence behind her.

"Hello, Hannah."

Oh my God.

"Francis."

She turned her head and, as clear as day, he was there. No remorse for what he did to her all those months ago – just a face as cold as stone.

"I assume you've come back to ask for your position on the team?" he sneered.

It was Hannah's turn to flash a signature smile. "No, actually. Erica asked me back herself."

Only Hannah could see the subtle change in his comfort level. "Oh. Did she now?"

"Yeah. I'm just about to do some freestyle now to warm up, so if you want to stay and watch then you are more than welcome to," Hannah said, admittedly condescendingly but feeling justified in doing so.

As Andrew returned to the sidelines and sat down on the bench, Francis joined him. "Let's see if you still have it, Han."

And oh, did Hannah still have it.

As the music played (a soft, tinkle of a piano and a violin could be heard swimming around the rink) she came to life, just as she always did when she was on the ice. It was strange to be skating where she never thought she would skate again... such familiar walls and people and sounds, yet she was different.

Her fan spirals made her want to scream *"I did it! I did it without you!"* and she knew she had nailed her flying sit spin when it felt like she was floating on air. She could physically feel herself keeping balanced in the air for as long as possible, to really give the sit spin a polished look. She didn't have to look back to know that Erica was impressed.

When the music stopped and Hannah came off the ice, Andrew stood up. "Fantastic job, Han. I'm just going to get some water, does anyone want anything?"

Erica stood up as well. "Me! I need a coffee. Come with me and I'll show you where the café is. You know, they do a delightful cocoa with whipped cream and marshmallows around this time of year..." her voice faded as she and Andrew walked out of the door and through the corridor to the café, while Hannah and Francis were left in the silence.

"She probably only went with him because she wanted to tell him what he could improve on," Francis said.

"Maybe," Hannah replied, "but she is really impressed with him. I think Andrew has made a new friend."

"He's not perfect, Han."

"None of us are perfect, Francis, not even you. But for an amateur I think Andrew is pretty good."

To this, Francis said nothing. *Erica must have already told him about Andrew's lack of skating experience,* she realized.

Suddenly, Francis sighed and rolled his eyes. "Are you still mad at me for replacing you?"

Somehow he always had to make it about him. "I was mad. I was mad for a very long time. But I've got Andrew now, and I think he's better for me than you were."

There was something in Francis' face that proved her response stung him a little bit. He looked up at her then, with sadness in his eyes. The eyes that used to melt Hannah like butter and make her do whatever he wanted.

"I was wondering. If you're not my partner anymore, then do you maybe want to hang out later? Get some food? I know this great place, the best in the surrounding area. My parents have connections."

That was it.

The moment that Hannah had been waiting for almost her whole life. The moment when Francis asked her out.

But what about Andrew?

"Um… I don't know. I might be a bit busy later…"

"Is Andrew your boyfriend or something? Because you know you aren't supposed to date your professional partner when you're under Erica's guidance. She'll kill you!"

Oh no oh no oh no. If Hannah told anyone that she and Andrew were more than friends, she wouldn't be able to train with Erica anymore. She couldn't take that risk.

Plus, after all of those years waiting for Francis to say something, she could understand why he waited until now, and she didn't begrudge him that sensible attitude at least.

"Okay. I suppose dinner would be nice. It would be good to catch up with you, you know? Hear what you've been doing with your life since last time we spoke."

"Cool," Francis said, "I'll text you later?"

"Sure, see you then…"

***

The restaurant that Francis chose was just as elaborate and expensive as he was. There were glass chandeliers on the ceilings, old portraits of gentry lining the walls, and candles in real candlesticks.

Hannah wore an outfit that she had had in her closet for a long time now – a purchase from her wild late teens that she thought would come in handy if Francis ever asked her out. She wore the black dress with matte black heels and a silver choker necklace with sophistication.

Francis played the gentleman and pulled out her chair for her so that she could sit down. He was dressed in a suit – the type her former fellow employees used to wear – but nonetheless he looked quite attractive.

What she did realize though, as soon as he flashed her one of those signature smiles, she didn't get butterflies like she used to. Instead, she felt sort of guilty about going out for a meal when it wasn't with Andrew. Hannah knew not to call it a date, because technically Francis had never said those exact words… but it didn't change the fact that it was a date. She should have been looking into Andrew's eyes, not the eyes of the guy who ditched her when she wasn't useful anymore.

Francis was as cool as a cucumber, leaning back on his chair and folding his arms around his chest, grinning at Hannah while she peered at the menu. She didn't know what half of the dishes were. It was all in French.

"I think I'll have the pizza."

Francis laughed patronizingly. "You can't order pizza! This is a reputable establishment."

Hannah raised an eyebrow. "Then why is pizza on the menu in the first place?"

Francis didn't have an answer for that, and so gave her a stare as if to say *stop talking before other people hear you.*

When the waiter took their order (Hannah ordered the pizza despite Francis' snobbish remarks) and walked away, Francis sat up in his chair a little bit and cleared his throat.

"I suppose you're wondering why I asked you here tonight."

Hannah was curious, but said, "Not really. I mean, I assumed it was for a general catch-up? We used to be close, you and I." She chuckled. "Unless when you saw me for the first time again today you realized your undying love for me?"

Francis smiled – something he didn't do all that often. "No, actually. Well, yes I wanted a catch-up, but no to the undying love thing. I have a proposal for you."

She giggled jokingly at the wording. "A proposal? I thought you didn't love me!"

He rolled his eyes and he was now smiling so widely that she could see his teeth, a rare sight for those who knew Francis. "I wanted to know if you'd consider becoming my skating partner again."

Hannah's smile faded and she felt like all of the fun was being sucked out of the evening by a skate-shaped vacuum cleaner.

"I can't."

His smile faded too. "Why not? We've skated before. We're perfect together."

"Except you ditched me for another girl while I was still in the hospital."

"And I'm sorry for that," he said, not looking sorry in the slightest, "but if you've got any chance of placing in the U.S. Championships then you've got to stick with me."

All Hannah could do was laugh in his face. She tried so hard not to, she really did. But she couldn't help herself. "I need you?" she asked, her voice raised as far as it could go in such a posh restaurant. "From the way Erica was talking about you it seems as though *you* need me. Lucy not good enough for you?"

Francis could tell he was drowning, and so tried to turn it around. "Look, she is fine. It's you I'm worried about. You need the best partner you can get so you have a chance of winning something, and Andrew is so not the guy to do it with. He doesn't know anything! He has no experience. Join me, and we can take the world by storm."

Hannah stood up and pushed her chair in, looking sternly at Francis. "Are you dramatic or what? You don't need to worry about me, thank you very much. And Andrew got Erica's approval so I'd think he'd be a fine partner."

She unhooked her shoulder bag from the chair, brought some bits and bobs in, and fixed it while she talked. "You know, you actually had me thinking that you'd changed for a second there, Francis. But why else would you take a girl to the fanciest restaurant you can think of? To try to get her to abandon her partner, just so you'd have a better chance of winning a medal! I don't want to be a part of your games. I'm out of here."

Storming out and leaving Francis on his own in the most expensive place in the city, she felt some more of the strange weight being lifted from her. All that she had wanted to say to Francis since he left her professionally, she finally got to say. And he finally got to hear.

Chapter 12

The next day at training, Hannah didn't speak to Francis once. Their paths crossed a couple of times – when they were warming up on the floor, quick glances from either end of the ice rink… but Hannah had no interest in being associated with him anymore. Their friendship was over, and their partnership was over.

It was a good thing that she didn't have lots of time to focus on Francis, because Erica had some news for her.

"Hannah! Andrew! There's something I forgot to tell you this morning."

Erica stepped on the ice while she was talking, flawlessly floating towards the pair of young skaters, who had been working on some pair lifts.

"Good news or bad news?" Hannah asked, curious as to what was so important that Erica interrupted their carry lifts. That was a tricky session – the bravery that she had to have, and the trust she had to have in Andrew to allow him to lift her that high, was possibly the hardest thing about skating. It wasn't that she didn't trust Andrew, but it was difficult to trust someone when so many people had let you down in the past.

"Exceptionally good news! So you know how you want to compete in the U.S. Championships?"

Andrew's ears perked up. "Wait — you mean we are allowed to compete?" He wore a smile of pure bliss, until Erica knocked him down.

"No. Not yet. But, there is a state championship competition, and I want you two to compete."

Hannah interrupted. "And when is this competition?"

Erica stayed quiet.

"Erica…"

She looked up at Hannah and Andrew, biting her lip. "Tomorrow."

Hannah and Andrew's mouths shot open at exactly the same time. "Tomorrow!" they shouted in unison.

"We can't do that, we're not ready." Andrew panicked, looking to Hannah like he was a deer trapped in the headlights.

"You can," Erica said calmly, "you have that routine that Hannah choreographed before I asked her back, and I've seen you both practicing it, so I know that it's good enough to compete with. You will have no problem going up against the other skaters in the state."

Hannah nodded. "Erica is right, Andrew. You know the routine, you are nailing all of the lifts, and there is nothing stopping us. Come on, let's do it. You want to go to the U.S. Championships as much as I do, and this is the only way in." Her stomach leaped in excitement for this opportunity – it was everything that she had been daydreaming about, as well as having nightmares about not doing.

Andrew sighed. "Okay. You're right; I do want this as much as you, but I just wasn't sure whether we were ready. That's all!"

Erica smiled. "Oh, you're a sensible guy, but you have no need to worry. You were born to skate, you know. I can see it when you're on the ice. It's time to compete."

***

It was the day of the state competition, and the crowd was already in good spirits. Music was echoing around the large rink to fill the gaps between each skating program, and the competition was about halfway done. Hannah and Andrew were next.

Hannah was dressed in a brand-new costume, its red velvet and silver sparkles illuminating her body, already making her look the part. Andrew had on a red shirt to match, with the shape of a rose sequined on, and they were both ready to go. Hannah's adrenaline levels were normal for the type of competition – she had done this type of thing before – but Andrew was a first-timer. His hands were shaking slightly, he had a distant look in his eyes, and he was starting to shiver.

Erica and Hannah noticed his anxious disposition and took him to the sidelines, where they managed to calm him down in less than a minute, Hannah rubbing his back so that the shivering would stop. All she wanted to do was to give him a hug and tell him that she believed in him. That everything was going to be great, because he was great.

Unfortunately, she didn't have time, because through the speakers came a familiar sound for Hannah, which meant it was time for action.

"Next up we have Hannah Avery and Andrew Mitcheson!"

And they took to the floor.

Hannah and Andrew did not skate to the song in the typical way. You could have heard a pin drop among the crowd as they performed side-by-side camel spins and they executed the throw jump in midair with excellence. The commentators were pleased too.

"And what a brave throw from Andrew there, Hannah responded especially well to the force behind it. What do you think, Wendy?" commented a male voice from the high box in the rink.

"Oh just fabulous, Jim. Andrew gets a little too close to the edges of the rink when he's roaming about, but Hannah keeps him in check."

When the music stopped, the majority of the crowd stood and applauded loudly, and Hannah and Andrew did the usual bowing routine, making sure to look the judges in the eye and giving them their best smiles. It had, after all, gone really well, so the smiles weren't fake.

As they came off the ice and the applause died down, Francis and a beautiful, petite girl passed them to make their way onto center ice. Hannah and Francis' eyes met for a split second, and they knew what the deal was. This was war.

Once everyone had skated, the judges took a break to deliberate on their final scores for each pair. While this was happening, the generic radio music was turned back on, and the crowd were too busy singing along to Taylor Swift to notice the cold stares that Francis and Hannah were giving each other.

There was a slight screech of a microphone and a cheery voice rang out. "Can all skaters please return to the ice? The final scores have been counted."

The rink turned into a crowded mess as multiple pairs of skates clambered on to the ice for a second time that evening. Some spectators were speaking to each other in hushed tones, but everyone on the ice was silent.

Jim and Wendy announced the scores. "Now, there are three places up for grabs at the U.S.

Championships. Those that place from first to third will be able to skate at such a prestigious event," Jim proclaimed.

Wendy took over the microphone. "Before we announce the results, we just want to say huge congratulations to all that took part. You are so talented and all deserve to go to the championships."

"In third place are Brad and Lillie."

The crowd cheered as two baby-faced skaters stood onto the podium and took their medals. *They're so young,* Hannah thought, *they must only be fifteen or sixteen.*

The rink went eerily quiet as partners grasped each other's hands and squeezed their eyes shut, as though they were saying a last-minute prayer.

"In second place are…"

The moment felt like it lasted for all eternity.

"… Hannah and Andrew!"

Some of the crowd gave a standing ovation and loud applause followed.

"Second place! We did it!" Andrew rejoiced as he turned to her and pulled her in for a warm hug, proceeding to drag her to the podium and proudly wear the medals.

Hannah was so happy, because it meant they made it to the U.S. Championships. But she knew what was coming next.

"And in first place, which is extremely well deserved… Francis and Lucy!"

"Oh crap," Hannah and Andrew said under their breath in unison. The U.S. Championships was going to be so much fun. Not.

And through the corner of her eye, smirking vindictively at her like the cat that got the metaphorical cream, was none other than Francis.

Chapter 13

A week flew by and it was time for the U.S. Championships.

Everything that Hannah had ever dreamed of was here, and everything was so different to how she had pictured this moment to be. Her accident, the frightening prospect of never being able to skate again, her partner of over a decade leaving her… it was so much to take in.

And yet, her life was so much better now. She had finally got rid of Francis who always put her down, she got some real-life experience working in a law firm, and her friendship with Anya was stronger than ever (they both regretted shouting at each other on the day of Hannah getting fired to the extent that they constantly bought each other flowers and chocolates to remind the other how much they adored them).

Plus, she had Andrew. Sweet, wonderfully supportive Andrew, who never made her feel worthless and always strived to do his very best for her. They have been sneaking intimate moments with each other while Erica wasn't looking; a squeeze of a hand on the resting benches, a quick peck on the cheek when one helped the other up from a nasty fall during training, and other silly things like that. She felt like a giddy teenager when she was with him, and he felt very much the same way.

Quite frankly, Erica was amazed at how well Andrew was doing. For an amateur, it was incredible how unnaturally quickly he picked up each move, and was always fairly cheerful when he got something wrong. Though, she supposed that was down to love.

Yes, Erica knew all about Hannah and Andrew. It came as no surprise to her when she caught a glimpse of them huddling on the benches after closing time at the rink, and staring into each other's eyes like they were scared to look away. It was easy to tell that they were in love, and she never questioned them about it. Usually she took a firm stand against partners on the ice who were partners in real life, because it hindered the strength of the skaters, but Hannah and Andrew's relationship made them two of the strongest skaters she had seen in all her years of coaching.

For the competition, Hannah was dressed in a bright yellow leotard, with an emblem of the sunshine drawn in sparkles on her left side where a pocket would go. In that same shade of yellow, Andrew was clad in a skating shirt that looked like it should go with a dinner jacket, and had a single yellow rose tucked into his shirt pocket. They knew what they had to do, and they were ready.

The ice rink was packed with hundreds of enthusiastic fans of skaters who were clinging to the edges of their seats every time the commentator announced a new skating act. Flowers and various teddy bears were thrown at the end of a program to signify that the people were supportive of the skaters from their own state, and while the skaters bowed and exited the rink, small children in matching outfits to their home team raced onto the ice and collected the presents. The stage was set.

Francis and Lucy skated before Hannah and Andrew, which sounded like a nightmare but turned out to be a relief, because Lucy made some silly mistakes and almost completely lost her footing on her corkscrew spin, for she was so nervous.

When they had finished their program, you could just about feel the severity of hatred that Francis had for Lucy. His eyes pretty much said it all.

"Lucy better watch out, or he'll turn her into a frog!" Andrew whispered, making Hannah almost spit out the water she was drinking from laughing so hard.

"Shhh! He'll hear you… and then he'll turn you into a frog too!" Hannah replied, making Andrew cover his mouth so no one could see how much he was enjoying this Francis-bashing moment.

"We're next on."

"Yeah, it won't be long. Bigger competitions like these usually have longer breaks in between each program. They just want to be sure on the scores before calling out the next skaters."

Andrew knitted his eyebrows together. "You're not nervous?"

Hannah looked up at him. "No."

"How can you not be? I thought this was all you ever wanted."

"It is. That's why I'm not nervous."

Andrew didn't have to ask any more questions. He just got it.

A noise snapped them out of their conversation. "And next up we have Hannah Avery and Andrew Mitcheson, skating a program to *Here Comes the Sun* by the Beatles." She had chosen such a fun song, and was going to have the time of her life.

The moment was here. And they were both ready.

Andrew squeezed Hannah's hand one last time before their fates were set. "I love you, Han."

Any nerves that she did have the second before they took to the ice popped like a bubble in her body, and she was left with pure bliss.

"I love you too, Andrew. Now, let's win this thing!"

When they took their places on the ice, her mind couldn't comprehend how large the rink actually was. Some people were lucky enough to train here, and she wished she could do the same in the future. The audience were looking expectantly at the pair, hoping for a show that they were never going to forget.

If they wanted it, that's what they were going to get.

Little darling, it's been a long cold lonely winter. Little darling, it feels like years since it's been here...

Hannah and Andrew skated so passionately, that the audience were immediately captivated. Andrew performed an overhead-rotational lift with Hannah, switching his hands at the perfect moment to catch Hannah while she was holding a pose, her eyes staring into the distance as if remembering all that she had worked for.

Here comes the sun, do, do, do, do, here comes the sun and I say, it's alright...

They did side-by-side shotgun spins, at exactly the right distance from each other so that they wouldn't hit each other with the blade of their skate. Their legs were at a flattering ninety-degree angle, making the spin look so elegant.

Little darling, the smiles returning to the faces...

Smiling, they linked hands and gazed into each other's eyes as they scanned the rink on their skates, preparing for their next lift. They didn't have to pretend they were happy for the routine – they just were.

Little darling, I feel the ice is slowly melting...

Andrew picked Hannah up and prepared for the twist lift, which sent her spinning horizontally. This was the winning lift, the one that had the crowd gasping with joy as they knew they were looking at the champions...

Until Andrew stumbled when trying to catch Hannah and she partially missed his arms, sending her landing awkwardly on the ice.

A familiar pain shot through Hannah's veins, and she knew.

Her leg was hurt again.

The music abruptly stopped and the interlude music was switched back on to try to cut out the sound of the people in the crowd panicking. From the sidelines, Erica and Francis winced and Erica rushed onto the ice when she realized what had happened. Andrew crouched down to stroke Hannah's forehead, telling her that everything was going to be alright, and how sorry he was for letting it happen. He rushed off the ice, and Hannah didn't mind, as she assumed he was going to alert the paramedic team.

But then they showed up, and Andrew didn't turn up with them.

What was going on?

"Hold on tight, Miss Avery, we're going to give you some pain relief for that leg. It doesn't look too serious, but you've irritated the leg that you've hurt before, so it will be hurting a lot right now."

When the pain had subsided ever so slightly, Hannah took some deep breaths and composed herself. *Andrew should be back by now,* she thought to herself. *So where is he?*

Resting on the benches at the sidelines, she scanned the room looking for Andrew. Just a few yards away, she spotted him. He seemed to be talking to an attractive young woman, who was in deep conversation with him and couldn't stop smiling.

And then it hit her like a ton of bricks. Andrew was ditching her, and already making other plans for possible future partners.

No way is this happening again. Hannah speed-walked (well, hobbled as quickly as she could with the temporary crutches that the paramedic team had provided her) over to where Andrew and this mystery woman were standing.

The young woman smiled and held out a hand, expecting a pleasant greeting. "Hi, Hannah, is it?"

"How the hell do you know my name? Who are you?"

Andrew interrupted her. "Han, there's no need to get defensive–"

"You do realize that you can't just go around stealing other people's partners as soon as one of them takes a fall? Because I'm strong, I've recovered from this leg injury before and I'll do it again. You cannot take Andrew away from me." Tears of anger welled in her eyes, an accusing finger pointing at this woman who she'd never seen before.

"I am so sorry for her behavior right now," Andrew chirped in. *He's sorry? For his betrayal!*

Slightly taken aback but overall very calm and composed, the woman looked up at Andrew. "That is perfectly fine; she has absolutely nothing to say sorry for. I understand what this looks like, Hannah, and I won't blame you for thinking that I was some young skater wanting to snap Andrew up for myself. With what Andrew has told me about your accident on the ice all those months ago, I would think the same too if I was in your shoes!"

Hannah calmed down a bit and the stinging sensation started to go from her eyes, enabling her to talk. "Then who are you?"

The woman smiled. "I was hoping you'd seen me in the audience so you wouldn't have got the wrong idea, but never mind. I'm Kaley Hill, the producer of *Skating with the Stars*."

Skating with the Stars was pretty much the best show for showcasing professional skaters on television.

Most Olympic skaters would sell their souls for a chance to appear on that show.

Realizing the full extent of her actions towards who she was talking to, she felt immediately guilty. "Oh my God, I am so sorry for my outburst earlier! I just thought…"

"I know what you thought; you don't have to explain yourself to me. Andrew has already told me everything."

"Wait – you've met before?"

Kaley looked bemused at Andrew. "You still haven't told her?"

It was Andrew's turn to explain himself. "I work for the television company that produces *Skating with the Stars*. Kaley is a good friend of mine, we've been in the business for a few years together, and once I'd met you I knew there was something about you that I couldn't let go of."

It was all starting to make sense to Hannah. "Wait – so is that why you pick up new skating moves so quickly?"

"Yeah… I probably should have told you that I'm good friends with many professional skaters that have been on the show and whenever we hang out we go skating, and they teach me stuff. It's hilarious; our idea of a fun night out is learning how to perfect a half-Biellmann spin."

"We don't need your life story, Andrew," Kaley laughed. "Let's cut to the chase. Would you like to become a permanent judge on our show? There's no actual skating involved – well, there certainly won't be for you for a good few months – but even when your leg is well rested, you can still be part of the skating world as a professional without having to put too much pressure on your leg. When you're well enough to skate, you can! But it gives you a chance to be a skater even when you're not skating. So what do you say? Want to join us on the team?"

Hannah was stunned. Again, it was one of those life-changing moments in her existence, but this one made it feel totally worth breaking her leg.

"Of course I will! And it's all because of you, Andrew. Thank you. You have brought so much to my life."

"Hold that thought…"

He ran around the rink and up to the judges' desk, whispering something to them. All four of the judges wasted no time in nodding their heads, and Hannah could just about see Andrew shaking their hands in grateful thanks.

Then, there was an announcement from the commentators.

"Ladies and gentlemen, may we now present Andrew Mitcheson, who has something very special to say to a very special girl. Would Miss Hannah Avery please take to the rink?"

All of a sudden, a spotlight fell on Andrew who was now standing in the center of the rink. Erica unexpectedly came to Hannah's side, and held on tight to her, the two of them stepping onto the ice. Erica supported Hannah all the way, making sure she didn't put any pressure on her leg.

When she came to a stop next to Andrew in the rink, he spoke through a microphone. His eyes went all dewy and he was pursing his lips.

"You are one of the most brilliant skaters I know. But more importantly, you are one of the most brilliant people I know. When I first saw you in that coffee shop, I instantly fell in love. And yes, I was kind of rude to you..."

"Kinda rude!" Hannah exclaimed, not sure where all of this was going, but smiling nonetheless. "You were the world's rudest flirt!"

Andrew bowed his head and chuckled. "I know! But it was only because I knew we were meant to cross paths, and I got scared. I get defensive when I'm scared, and so come across as kind of an idiot. Anyway, what I wanted to say was that I love you; always have, always will. And I want to share the rest of my life with you, on and off the ice."

Hannah still didn't know what was going on, but started to understand when Andrew got down on one knee.

"Hannah Avery, my ice princess, will you consider becoming my ice queen?"

He used his free hand to take a small cubed box out of his pants pocket, flipping it open to reveal a ring that looked like it had been carved out of ice, with the most gorgeous diamond resting in the middle.

She couldn't believe it! Shaking slightly from the surprise (and also the pain in her leg, but she wasn't thinking about that), she let a single tear roll down her cheek as she couldn't stop smiling.

"Yes."

The audience erupted into a standing ovation. Erica hugged Hannah in congratulations and let her go when Andrew pulled her into an embrace, holding her tightly so that she wouldn't fall. Leaning upwards to kiss her fiancé, she thought back to how she wouldn't have even known Andrew if it weren't for her accident, and for the only time in her life, she felt grateful for breaking her leg. After all, all things happened for a reason, didn't they?

What to read next?

If you liked this book, you will also like *The Stolen Bride*. Another interesting book is *Taming the Billionaire*.

The Stolen P

Lindsey Thomas is at the top
successful career, fabulous ~~~
Crawford, her wonderful fiancé, her lif~
she wants it. That is, until Patrick dumps her th~
of their engagement party. Brokenhearted, Lindsey
heads to her best friend Kate's family beach house to
heal, as it is temporarily vacant and she hopes some
alone time at the beach will help her feel better. But
when Kate's brother, novelist Harris Welling, shows
up unexpectedly, things get complicated. Harris
insists that she stay at the house as he is only there to
get some work done before the rest of the family
arrives the following week, and Lindsey agrees,
despite her reservations. Lindsey soon finds herself
drawn to her best friend's handsome older brother.
So soon after her disastrous breakup, she tries her
best to resist the growing chemistry between them,
but she cannot deny her feelings and a relationship
quickly develops. However, when Patrick pops back
into her life unexpectedly wanting to be with her
again, she is forced to make a choice ... but will she
make the right one?

Taming the Billionaire

Kate Hensley sells her handmade soap on the internet and works in her best friend's bar to make ends meet. When a new resort comes to her hometown, she takes a chance and schedules a meeting with the CEO to get her soaps in the resort. What she doesn't plan on is the CEO, Luke Wilder, being so handsome and very arrogant. A chance encounter resulting in a fender bender gets them off on the wrong foot and she thinks that she'll never get her foot in the door. But when they happen to meet again, they end up apologizing to each other and to Kate's surprise Luke asks her out on a date. Suddenly Kate's life goes from strictly business to whirlwind dates with the handsome CEO. She enjoys his company and it isn't long before her heart is lost to him. Just when she thinks everything is going right in her life, she finds out something that may destroy it all.

About Olivia West

Olivia West is a bestselling romance author who is known for her captivating stories with interesting characters, unusual settings, adventurous plots and intriguing relationships. In each of her stories she tries to make readers see in their imagination a mental movie in which they can feel emotions of the characters and are curious about what will happen next.

One Last Thing…

If you believe that *Love on Ice* is worth sharing, would you spend a minute to let your friends know about it?

If this book lets them have a great time, they will be enormously grateful to you – as will I.

Olivia

www.OliviaWestBooks.com

Made in the USA
Las Vegas, NV
02 December 2020

11931164R00085